CW01642894

GATORS

BY ERIC S BROWN

SEVEREDPRESS

GATORS

WWW.SEVEREDPRESS.COM

ISBN: 978-1-923165-74-8

GATORS

"This sucks," Aaron grumbled, slogging through the water of the swamp. It was up to his waist and tepid. Leaves and other debris floated by him on its surface.

Phil couldn't argue. He wasn't loving being out here in the dead of night either. Not the sort to vocally complain like Aaron, the frown he wore said it all for him.

The two of them were a few yards ahead of Chris and Steven. The objective of their four man squad was supposed to be learning how to navigate and move quickly in this type of environment.

Consulting his compass, Phil confirmed that they were still heading north though he didn't honestly have a clue as to how much ground had already been covered and how much farther there was left to go. What he did know was their march through the swamp was taking forever. There was no means of double timing it out here without running the risk of injury. The water for the most part was only around four feet deep at worst thus far but their pre-exercise briefing cautioned that it could sharply drop off to as deep as nine feet without warning.

All of them were armed with M16A2 rifles, the standard issue weapon for many National Guard units. For this exercise, their rifles were loaded with live rounds but they didn't have clearance to fire any rounds. Phil was the only one wearing a sidearm for the exercise. A SIG M18 was holstered on his belt. Not that there was anything much to shoot at out here. Rationally, Phil knew that most of the snakes in the swamp were non-venomous and not Cottonmouths but he was still scared. As a young boy, he'd run into a pair of Cottonmouths with his uncle while out hunting and the experience left its mark on him. The things were hiding under a partly submerged log and when his uncle moved it, the Cottonmouths had struck, one biting into the upper thigh of his right leg and the other just above his knee on the left. Phil would never forget how his uncle screamed, grabbing and prying loose one of the snakes then the other, bashing them into the log until they were dead. Dripping with sweat and wide eyed from the pain of the venom pumping through him, Phil's uncle had managed to get them out of the swamp to the road before passing out. Phil called for help with the jeep's radio but then could only watch as his uncle lay twitching until help arrived. . . and it had arrived too late. His uncle's death had been horrid and sickening, his legs swelling and bloating up, the muscles of his face taut and drawing up. The sight haunted Phil through the rest of his youth and he had kept as far away from swamps as possible. Tonight, he hadn't a choice though. Orders were orders.

"Hell yeah, it sucks!" Steven shouted out his agreement with Aaron's assessment of their situation.

"Keep it down," Phil snapped.

Steven shot him a ticked off look. "Why? Ain't nothing out here that can hear me, buddy, except for the birds and gators."

"Damn it, Steven," Phil shook his head. "If this were real and not an exercise. . ."

"But it's not, man," Steven reminded him.

This was Phil's first time out as the squad's C.O. Up until yesterday all four of them had been the same rank and Steven clearly had issues with him as their squad leader. Phil knew he needed to nip that crap in the bud before it got out of hand or his superiors became aware of it, but wasn't quite sure how to handle it yet.

"Steven," Chris said. His tone was as hard and cold as ice. If there was anyone in their little squad that you didn't want to mess with, it was him. "Shut the hell up."

Phil saw Steven flinch at the anger clearly evident in Chris' reaction. It was his job as C.O. to keep Steven in line. Chris butting in, even if it was in support of his new position, still rankled him as much as Steven's disrespectful mouthing off.

"Look, guys," Phil said, motioning for Aaron to stop so that Chris and Steven could catch up to them. "None of us want to be out here but that's the job. Slog through hellholes like this, sweat our butts off, and go home smelling worse than crap. . .we all knew that was part of it when we signed on. We just gotta put together and do what we're told."

Steven looked as if he wanted to make some smart comment again but Chris hadn't stopped glaring at him.

"Don't get any ideas about this being a democracy," Phil went on. "I'm in command here so when I say jump, you ask how high. You guys crystal on that?"

"Yes sir," the others answered.

Phil allowed himself a small grin. "Good. Now come on. I want to get out of this place just as much as the rest of you."

And not one of them knew just how much that statement was true, Phil thought. Every time he saw something move in the water or the tall grass, it took all the control he had not to panic. Phil was afraid that if he did see a Cottonmouth or Water Moccasin his fear would take over and he would either run or blow the fragging snake to pieces with his M16.

Aaron took point as they started north again with Phil following right behind him. Chris fell back to take up the rear position trailing along after Steven. They were all silent. The swamp wasn't though. Around them, crickets chirped, frogs called out, and the water sloshed as they stroked through it.

At first, Phil thought his eyes were playing a trick on him. Something huge surfaced in the distance only to sink back into the murky water of the swamp. Ripples flowed out from the spot where it disappeared.

Freezing up ahead of him, Aaron asked, "What in the hell was that?"

"You saw it too?" Phil frowned.

"I sure did," Aaron nodded. "It was too big to miss."

"Hey," Steven said, catching up to them. "What's the hold up?"

"There's something in the water," Aaron answered.

Steven made a face. "What? A snake? A gator?"

"We don't know what it was," Phil said. "It was

damn big though. Too big to be a gator and sure as hell too big to be a snake."

"You sure?" Steven eyed Phil and Aaron. "Snakes can get pretty damn big in swamps like this."

"It had to be a gator," Aaron kept his eyes on the water.

"Why is that even a problem?" Steven cocked his head sideways. "We got live rounds. It comes up and bam, the sucker is gone."

"You're wrong," Chris growled.

"What are you talking about?" Steven whirled about. "I read that you can kill the things with even a .22 round or at worst a few 9mm shots."

"You read. . ." Chris gritted his teeth.

"Yeah, I read," Steven found the courage to talk back to him.

"Then you didn't read close enough," Chris shook his head.

"I grew up around here, guys," Aaron announced. "That whole bit about a .22 round killing a gator is when one of them has been caught and roped. . .a point blank shot to a soft spot on a gator's head. As to the 9mm, pretty much the same. Gators aren't as easy to kill as the internet might tell you. You get one of them coming at you, moving instead of captured, and it's a whole different ball game. They ain't bulletproof but the things are killing machines that you better not be hunting if you don't know what you're doing."

"Guys," Phil got their attention. "I say we just get the hell on out of here."

Chris grunted his approval while Aaron nodded.

"I thought that was the plan anyhow," Steven cackled. He took off walking, taking point in front of Aaron. For all his bravado though, Steven had the safety of his rifle off and held the weapon ready in an easy firing position.

Aaron and Phil let him take the lead without argument. It was clear Chris didn't give a crap who was on point as long as the group was moving forward. The sooner they were out of the swamp, the better, that was his bottom line.

The water in front of Steven exploded upwards. There was a flash of something olive gray and massive, then. . .Steven was gone from their sight, below the waterline. There was intense splashing as presumably Steven struggled for his life.

"Get the hell back!" Chris shouted. "And spread out!"

Phil knew he should have been the one giving those orders. All he could manage to do though was stare helplessly at the rolling water.

"Oh God!" Aaron called on a higher power for

help in a state of utter dismay.

Blasting away at the water would only kill Steven too. . .if he wasn't dead already. It was a chance that Phil couldn't let them take.

"Don't shoot!" Phil barked.

"Then what the hell are we supposed to do?" Aaron demanded to know, his voice nothing short of a desperate shriek.

The muddy water had turned red. Whatever had a hold of Steven was tearing him apart or it sure seemed like it.

"Screw it," Chris roared, opening up with his M16. Blasting away on full auto, he hosed the disturbance in the water with hot lead. When Chris stopped firing, the water was still. Pieces of Steven bobbed up to the surface.

Phil felt bile rise up in his throat and had to look away. One of Chris' legs floated in the red and brown murk of the swamp. Not even a full foot away from it was his head. All the flesh and hair on one side had been slashed away and the bone crumpled. Phil had seen brain matter in the glimpse he'd gotten. His body heaved despite his effort not to vomit and his breakfast burst from his mouth, splashing into the water.

"Holy. . ." Aaron squealed, backpedaling even more away from where the pieces of Steven floated.

Chris' M16 clicked empty. He ejected the weapon's spent magazine, slapping a fresh one into place.

“Stay sharp!” Chris yelled, pointing the barrel of his M16 back towards the water around him.

Something huge and gray burst up from the water. Chris' M16 roared, spitting bullets at point blank range, but they did nothing to save him. The gator was larger than any Phil had ever heard of. Its head tilted, the thing's mouth closing on Chris about his waist. The power of its jaws crushed Chris' midsection, nearly cutting him in two. The massive beast went under again, taking Chris with it.

“Run!” Phil heard himself screaming. “Get out of the water!”

Aaron didn't need to be told twice. He bolted alongside Phil, running full out for the shore. The requirement of their training to stay in the swamp's water utterly forgotten. The exercise was over. It was do or die time now.

Aaron reached the shore first, turning around, M16 ready to offer cover if needed. Phil lunged out of the water next to him. Looking back there was no sign of Chris or the massive gator, if that was actually what the thing was.

“That thing was enormous!” Aaron's eyes were wide with stark terror.

"No! Really?" Phil snapped.

"You think it's still out there?" Aaron asked.

"How the hell should I know?" Phil's hands were trembling but he was determined to keep his composure. Staying calm and clear headed was their only hope of getting out of the swamp alive.

"Maybe. . .maybe it was just hungry and it's full now," Aaron said as if reassuring himself.

Phil realized that they were treating the gator as if it were a shark or something and started backing away from the shoreline.

"I don't want to risk it, do you?" Phil asked.

Aaron saw Phil retreating and joined him.

The monster came out of the muddy, murky water like a rocket. It was somehow even larger than Phil had thought it was. The thing had to be at least twenty feet long and its head was a solid four feet above the ground. Phil saw at once that the thing was unlike any gator he'd ever seen. It was clearly a gator at its core though. The thing's body shape was as it should be except for being overly large. The differences were in its scales and eyes. The gator's scales looked harder and thicker, like armor covering its body, and some of them were spiked. Its eyes glowed a bright shade of red as if there were fires burning within them.

Aaron tried to hurl himself from the thing's path

but it was just too fast despite its size. Its huge jaws clamped together severing his left leg at the hip in an explosion of blood. Howling in pain, Aaron fell. He landed roughly on his back, somehow still conscious. The impact sent his M16 flying from his grasp. The huge gator didn't stop. As it came on farther up the shore towards Phil, one of its feet came down on Aaron. The gator's weight caved in Aaron's ribs. They cracked, snapping beneath his flesh and tearing through it, killing him instantly. As it kept moving one of its rear feet stomped on Aaron's head.

"Back the hell off!" Phil screamed at the gator, opening up with his M16. Bullets struck the scales of its back and shoulders, sparking as they made contact and bouncing harmlessly away. They didn't even slow the beast.

There was more distance between the beast and Phil than there had been for Aaron. He was able to avoid its charge if just barely. As the huge gator barreled on past him, Phil kept firing, pouring bullets into its side hoping to get better penetration and actually do some harm.

The huge, messed up alligator-thing snapped about in his direction as Phil ejected his rifle's spent magazine, desperately trying to reload. He screamed as the gator charged him again. This time, there was no escape. Powerful jaws closed on Phil, breaking bones, teeth rending flesh, as the gator carried him from the shore. Phil's cries became sickening gargles as he disappeared with the gator beneath the murky water of the swamp.

****

When most people think of Florida, they tend to think of the cities or the beaches. Gary knew he certainly was guilty of that. The realty agent he'd reached out to introduced him to the more rural parts of the state, the wide open country and the swamp lands around them. The guy had sold him on a small, one bedroom house, that he could afford to triflat out pay cash for.

It took two weeks to tie up all the loose ends of the life Gary was leaving behind. There hadn't been anything easy about it either. The end of his ten year marriage had hurt like hell and that was why Gary needed to get away, put as much distance between himself and his ex-wife as possible. His future lay in starting over, completely and utterly, with no ties to his past. Gary knew that was the only way he would be able to heal and eventually be okay.

Gary pulled into the driveway of the house. The place was just as secluded as the agent told him it would be. There was flat, green land that stretched to the horizon to the north and west while to the east and south a few houses and the edge of Trenton Swamp could be seen. It was everything Gary had asked for. The house was close to 800 square feet in size. It was quaint and nondescript, old too. The paint of its exterior walls was flaking in spots but Gary figured that would be easy enough to fix up. The roof was metal though and not only intact but sturdy looking as well. Gary was thankful for the few trees to each side of the driveway that gave him at least a feeling of some privacy. Not that he really needed to worry about people out here. His place was a solid ten minute drive from the streets of the closest town and his only neighbors were the handful of houses to the south between Trenton Swamp and his home.

Shoving the gear shift into park and shutting off the car's engine, Gary stepped out into the hot rays of the midday, Florida sun. He stood there for a moment, sweat already beginning to bead on his skin, looking up at the clear, blue sky above. The air was a sharp contrast to the air conditioner provided coolness inside his car. Mentally kicking himself into action, Gary moved to pop open the trunk. The bags waiting for him there were as meager as his house. One suitcase, one metal briefcase, and a pair of duffel bags. He was able to get them all out and carry them up to the tiny set of steps leading up to the house's porch and front door. Gary sat aside the suitcase, with two duffel bags dangling from his shoulder, so that he could dig the key out of his pants pocket. Hurriedly, Gary fumbled the door open.

Sunlight spilled into the house through the living room window that ran most of the length of its driveway side. As he walked in, Gary noticed the couch, chair, and large TV the former owner had left behind. They'd come with the house as part of its price along with other furnishings like the washer and dryer in the washroom between the kitchen and the house's rear door, the bed for the single bedroom, and the microwave, stove, and refrigerator in the kitchen itself. It made his life easier and saved him the time of getting all of it bought and set up himself.

Gary walked into the bedroom, setting his duffel bags and suitcase on the floor. He gently tossed the metal briefcase on the bed and leaned over to open its locks. Flipping up the lid, Gary looked down on the disassembled AXSR inside. The rifle had been with him a long, long time. It was multi-caliber, extremely durable and dependable, crazy long ranged, and high powered as he'd spent a great deal having it modified to fire .50 caliber rounds. The rifle had once even survived a fall out of a helicopter during his tour in the Sandbox. The weapon was a thing of beauty despite the scars it had picked up over the years. With a heavy sigh, Gary closed the suitcase and sat on the bed, lowering his face into the palms of his hands.

When he had married Eva, she'd thought he was a traveling, corporate consultant. Gary managed to keep up the facade right up until the end and until that moment where she discovered what he truly did for a living the two of them were fine. Once Eva figured it out though, that was the end. She was unable to condone how he made the money that paid for her expensive shopping sprees and their home that was as close to a mansion as he could allow without overly drawing too much attention to them. Gary vividly remembered one of their last arguments in which Eva actually threw a vase at him like in a scene from an old cheesy, crime movie. She demanded he give it up, quit and find some other way to make money. He could see that Eva still loved him very much but knew he could never give up his trade. Killing was all he knew. It was the only talent God had blessed him with.

Gary had gone straight from high school into the army. There he'd eased his way up the ranks and into the special forces and ultimately into a black ops squad that got all the dirty jobs. He loved America and killing in her name was justifiable and he didn't lose sleep at night over it. The C.I.A. recruited him and paid a hell of a lot better. As the missions became more and more questionable though under a liberal and corrupt regime. . .Gary had gotten out, leaving the military behind and went into business for himself. The years of killing left him well prepared to get in, take out a target, and leave no trace or clue to his identity behind. It wasn't as hard to get started as one might think it would be. His time traveling the globe, making hits in the name of king and country, left him with a plethora of contacts to discreetly make use of. In seemingly no time at all, he was one of the most sought after hit men on the planet. All it had taken though was one slip up at home for Eva to discover what his job really was. Part of him wondered if his own subconscious was behind it happening, moved to do so by some suppressed guilt from not being honest with Eva. Regardless, the discovery changed everything.

It was fortunate that Eva still loved him, very much so, and that he trusted her. Had he not seen the loyalty and love in her eyes that remained even after she'd decided to throw him out, there would have been no choice but to make her disappear.

Doing that would have destroyed him. Sure, she was ticked. She'd never forgive him or be civil to him again but even so Gary knew too that Eva would never expose him. That saved her life. He missed her like hell. Their years together were the best of his life and Gary was well aware that he wouldn't ever find a love like what they had shared again. There would forever be a hole in his heart that couldn't be repaired.

Now, here he was in Florida, alone, with very little to his name. Gary had signed over pretty much everything beyond the funds for his new home and a bit of money to keep him going until his next job to Eva. And he wasn't ready to take on a new job yet. His head was too screwed up. In his line of work, a single mistake could leave you dead or behind bars. Gary had to get himself together before taking on another contract and it was his hope that being so far away from Eva, the city they had lived in, and being here alone would do the trick of getting himself back into focus.

Rather than start unpacking, Gary leaned back to sprawl out on the bed. He stared up at the ceiling trying to drive away his thoughts of Eva and then closed his eyes. The exhaustion of the drive had taken a larger toll on him than he'd thought and sleep came quickly.

****

The sun was past its zenith in the sky as Sheriff Peterson spat into the murky water of the swamp. He wasn't supposed to be out here, that's what he told himself anyway. Feeling too old for the crap he was dealing with, Sheriff Peterson wanted to be at home, sitting at the dinner table across from Martha, and enjoying some fried chicken and gravy before collapsing into his easy chair in front of the TV and catching up on the latest episodes of Alone. Sheriff Peterson wasn't an outdoors survivalist but had always wanted to be. Steepling his fingers together, he cracked their joints loudly.

"Sheriff?" Stacia Flynn, his lead deputy, looked around at him with an expression of concern on her supermodel-like, angular face. "You okay?"

"This crap always seems to go down when it's time to head home, doesn't it, Stacia?" Sheriff Peterson grumbled. "And this one. . .this takes the whole damn cake and then some."

Stacia didn't respond so he took her silence as unspoken agreement.

A pair of teenage kids who'd come out here, most likely to smoke some weed they bought off a dealer at school, had found the bodies. The experience had scared the holy hell out of them. They had still been pale and trembling when he arrived on the scene to question them himself. After releasing the two of them and marching out into the swamp where the bodies were, Sheriff Peterson saw at once why the kids were so shaken. The national guardsman on the shore no longer had a head. Not really. His skull was crushed flat, eye balls mashed and gooey out of their sockets. Fragments of white, broken bone pierced the flesh of the distorted features of the man's face in numerous areas. The man's chest and ribs weren't in much better shape. It was equally crushed and pressed into the soft ground. The body was also missing one of its legs. The corpse was bad enough that even he had gagged at the sight of it but there was more. Stacia, along with two other of his deputies, Doug and Zack, had also fished numerous body parts from the muddy water just off the bank where they now stood. The body parts were spread out so that they could all be seen though Sheriff Peterson could imagine how they would have bobbed up and down in the water when the kids discovered them. He shuddered despite himself and hoped that Stacia hadn't noticed.

Sheriff Peterson cleared his throat and said, "I see three arms. You wanna tell me exactly how many people we got dead out here?"

"We're guessing four based on the remains,"

Stacia answered. "You know how the Guard loves their bureaucracy. They wouldn't give us any more info than they had to and claim to have an officer on the way out here to talk with us."

"Great," Sheriff Peterson shook his head. "Just freaking great."

All hope of making it home at any decent hour had died and been wiped out of existence.

Stacia gestured at the bodies. "From the looks of things, these guys were attacked in the water though two of them made it onto the shore, not that doing so did them any good. Whatever killed their buddies came right on up after them."

"What gets me, Sheriff, is that these guys were armed," Zack commented. "And I don't mean with peashooters either."

Zack leaned over to pick up an M16 and show it to him. "Sheriff, these guys were trained soldiers carrying military gear. Whatever took them out had to have hit them hard and fast, without much warning. Even so, you can see from the shell casings scattered around that they did manage to put up a fight. Ain't nothing I know of out here that can stand up to the type of firepower these guys were packing."

Sheriff Peterson chuckled. "What? You telling me we got ourselves an honest to God swamp monster out here?"

"No sir," Zack replied quickly. "I'm only telling you that I don't have a clue what could have done this."

"The tracks whatever this thing left don't help identify it either," Stacia pointed out. "They're sort of like gator tracks but. . ."

"Yeah," Sheriff Peterson nodded, cutting her off. "I got eyes, ya know? They're way too big to be a gator unless Zack's right and we do really have some sort of monster to worry about."

Sheriff Peterson reached into his pocket for the pack of cigarettes he carried to ease his nerves in cases as gory and messed up as this one. He lit up and sucked in a deep drag of smoke, exhaling slowly.

"I reckon the first thing we need to do is get what's left of these poor bastards to the morgue so Dr. Jeffery can look them over. We can drag the water for the rest of them later," Sheriff Peterson said. "See if we can get our own IDs on them and if we're lucky find out what did this."

The sound of footfalls sucking in the mud caught Sheriff Peterson's attention. He turned to see a live guardsman marching towards them.

"Oh God help us," Sheriff Peterson muttered too quietly for anyone but Stacia to hear.

"Sheriff!" the man bellowed. "I'm Sergeant Major Jenkins."

The sergeant major was one hell of a big man. He stood around six foot one and Sheriff Peterson put his weight at well over two hundred. It wasn't fat though like you might expect to see on an officer of his age and rank, the pounds were all hard muscle. The sergeant major's dark hair was flecked with gray and he had to be pushing fifty.

"Peterson," he responded, reluctantly extending a hand to the sergeant major. "We weren't expecting you to make it out here so soon."

"When you find out four of your boys are dead, Sheriff, one tends to hustle a bit," Sergeant Major Jenkins said without any humor in his voice.

"I feel ya," Sheriff Peterson grunted. "You wanna tell us what your boys were up to wading around this swamp?"

"They were on a training exercise, Sheriff," Sergeant Major Jenkins frowned.

Sheriff Peterson saw him catch sight of what was left of his people for the first time.

"Oh lord," the sergeant major managed to get out before turning and dropping to his knees. Sheriff Peterson watched the man throw up his lunch onto the mud. When the heaving stopped, the sergeant major wiped at his mouth.

"Here," Zack said, offering him a hand up back onto his feet.

The sergeant major took it gladly.

"What the hell happened to them?" Sergeant Major Jenkins asked.

"Honestly," Sheriff Peterson shrugged, "At this point, your guess is as good as ours."

"We think some kind of animal attacked them," Zack added.

The sergeant major's eyes bugged at that.

"Yeah," Sheriff Peterson was sympathetic to what had to be going through his head. "We don't have a clue as to what sort of animal either. We're gonna find out though and hunt the thing down. You can count on that."

"Glad to hear it, Sheriff," Sergeant Major Jenkins managed a weak smile. "These boys were good soldiers trying to serve their country. They didn't deserve to go out like this."

****

"*Well, it's all right, riding around in the breeze,*" the stereo belted out as Tom's car cruised along the old road, windows down. The road was bumpy as hell but he didn't mind. His mind was on larger things. . .better things. If things worked out, he could be looking at a Pulitzer Prize. Tom smirked at that thought. At least a promotion anyways, that much was for sure. The tip he'd gotten was a trustworthy one. All that needed to be done was to validate it and get some pictures as evidence.

Tom started out at WXTV as an intern. With his charming demeanor and handsome looks, the rise to becoming part of the news staff was quick and easy. He had spent his first two years at the station doing mostly fact checking work and filler bits. This was his big shot. When Tom told his boss, Mr. Lawson, about the tip, the forty-something news editor nearly fell out of his chair. Tom thought the man might have been on the verge of having a heart attack. His cheeks flushed and Tom could swear the man was almost drooling. Tom couldn't blame him. If the tip was real and played out WXTV would be breaking exclusive news that would change how folks looked at the enormous, corporate power of Florida's Beckham Chemicals forever. The company spent huge amounts of money on public relations every year, bought and owned numerous politicians on both sides, donated to all the right places, and most certainly got the right folks to turn their heads when need be.

Beckham Chemicals produced everything from run of the mill water treatment and industrial compounds to supposedly, on the dark web, even bio-weapons. None of that mattered to Tom. What he cared about was how the company was skirting the E.P.A. requirements on how to handle its waste products. There were rumors that went back a decade or more about the corporation illegally dumping them in Florida's swamps. Now, if his anonymous source was telling the truth, Tom knew where one of the supposed dump sites was. Of course, he was going to need help getting to it. The site was accessible by car, being out in the secluded back areas of Trenton Swamp.

Having called ahead and using a WXTV company credit card, Tom hired a guide who could take him straight to the site or so he hoped. Turning off his music, Tom glanced at the screen of his GPS. He was almost there. Up ahead on the right of the road was a building that looked to be little more than a beat up shack. A weathered and faded sign over its door read “Joe Bob's Tours.”

Slowing, Tom pulled into the small gravel lot in front of it. He could see waters of the swamp beyond the shack and the little dock that had a couple of boats secured to it. Killing the engine, Tom got out of the car. A shaggy haired, deeply tanned man was already emerging from the shack to meet him.

“You the reporter that called?” the man asked,

voice husky and eyes keenly focused on him.

"That's me," Tom said, walking to meet him and extending a hand in greeting. "You must be Joe Bob."

The man gave a grunt. "Joe Bob was my dad. Folks around here just call me Junior."

"Everything ready?" Tom tried to keep his composure as his nose caught a whiff of Junior and he wondered if the man had ever taken a bath in his life.

"The boat's gassed up and the sun's high," Junior nodded. "Get your gear loaded and we'll get on with it."

Junior seemed almost as eager as he was to get underway.

"We in a hurry?" Tom opened the trunk of his car, grabbing up his camera bag.

"Trust me, city boy," Junior said, "It would be best if we were back before it gets dark and where you're wanting to go is a ways off."

Tom turned to stare at Junior with a questioning expression. "That so?"

"Damn well is," Junior huffed. "Lots of bad things out there in the swamp. Most of them come out mainly at night. The less chance we got of running into them, the better."

Junior led him down the dock and they climbed

into the motor boat. Tom placed his gear at his feet in front of him and settled into the seat Junior indicated that he take. Junior took his place at the boat's engine and loosened the boat from the dock.

“Gonna be a hot one today, city boy,” Junior informed him. “Hope you brought some bug repellent with you. The skeeters will be out for blood.”

Junior wasn't wrong about the heat. The sun was bright in the sky and its rays so hot Tom felt like he was being cooked alive. Within minutes of being on the water, his skin was slicked with sweat. Tom reached into his bag and took out a bottle of water he'd tossed into the camera bag while packing it. Twisting off its top, he gulped a good portion of it down.

“Why you wanting to go out so far, anyway?” Junior asked over the sound of the boat's motor, breaking the silence between them. “Ain't nothing to see but snakes, gators, and foul water.”

Tom wondered if telling Junior what he was up to was a good idea or not, deciding against it. “Does it matter?”

Junior grinned, showing off tobacco stained teeth. “No. I guess it don't.”

Several hours passed as Junior guided the boat deeper and deeper in the murk of Trenton Swamp.

They didn't talk a lot and when they did it wasn't about anything meaningful or important. That suited Tom just fine. He spent his time taking in the dark, somewhat ominous, haunting beauty of the swamp. Every once in a while Tom would catch sight of a heron rising into the air, disturbed by the boat's motor or a turtle resting on a log. He didn't get outdoors much, or ever really, and such sights were new and exciting to him.

The sun was sinking in the sky and the swamp thick about them as Junior carefully navigated the boat into an even darker part of the swamp. Trees lined the shores around the boat and the atmosphere was muggy and oppressive as if the swamp was attempting to smother them.

"That up there is where you're wanting to go," Junior gestured on up ahead. "Hedon's Cove. Just be quick about whatever it is you're up to. I want to be sure we're out of here before night falls."

Junior's apparent fear for the cove put Tom on guard. Before he'd put it off as being just a show for outsiders like himself. Now hearing the real emotion in Junior's voice, he wasn't so sure. Maybe there really was something to be afraid of out here.

As Junior steered them into the cove, Tom's eyes went wide. Right there in front of them was exactly what he had come looking for. It was as if no one even tried to hide what they were doing. A trio of barrels sat sinking into the mire close to the shore, abandoned there. Two of them were cracked. Putrid, brown fluid leaked from them into the water.

"I can't believe it," Tom blurted out. "I just can't believe it. Did you know these were here?"

"Nah," Junior shook his head. "Seen stuff like them out here before though. Given time they'll sink down and no one will ever know they were there to begin with."

"Do other people around here know about this?" Tom asked.

"I told you, city boy," Junior huffed. "Most people have the brains to stay the hell away from Hedon's Cove. Too many come out here and just vanish, never to be seen again."

Tom dug around in the camera bag, producing a small gadget.

"What's that?" Junior asked.

"It's a Gieger counter," Tom answered, turning it on.

A high pitched, pulsating crackle came from the Gieger counter.

"Stop the boat," Tom ordered.

Frowning, Junior did as he was told, halting their forward motion as best as he could.

"That thing reads radiation, right?" Junior was

staring at the Gieger counter. "All that noise, does it mean. . .?"

"Yes it does," Tom nodded frantically. "That cove is hot as hell."

Junior went pale.

"Calm down," Tom switched off the counter. "There's for sure radiation but I don't think it's anywhere near lethal levels, just a lot more than there should be. I mean there's some degree of radiation everywhere. As long as we don't hang around too long or get whatever is leaking out of those barrels on us, I think we'll be fine."

Junior didn't appear to really believe him. "You're gonna pay me more for this."

Tom knew he wasn't asking, he was stating a fact.

"Sure," Tom agreed, knowing his boss would happily sign off on doing it given the epic-ness of the story he'd be delivering. "I just need some photos of those barrels and we can go."

Slipping the camera from its bag, Tom hefted the Nikon and got it ready.

Junior whistled. "Now that's a camera."

Tom chuckled. "I don't own it. It belongs to the station I work for."

"But you know how to use it?" Junior was looking around.

"Well enough," Tom nodded, aiming the camera at the barrels.

"We ain't alone," Junior said. "There's something. . ."

The something huge hit the bottom of the boat like a torpedo. The bottom of the boat ruptured, pieces of wood and metal exploding upward. The shrapnel ripped at the two of them. Junior died instantly as a piece of it stuck him under his chin and went through his skull. The sharp end of the large splinter of wood protruded from the top of his head as Junior slumped over. For Tom, it was his legs that took the worst of it as he was flung backwards. His back thudded against the rim of the boat causing a fresh surge of pain to tear through him. Tom rolled with the impact keeping from being knocked out of the boat. He recovered enough to haul himself up onto his seat again only to see that the boat was quickly filling with muddy water through the large hole that whatever struck it had left in its wake. Tom looked down at the ragged, bleeding mess of his legs. They were badly sliced up with splinters of wood sticking out of them in several places. Tom didn't have a clue in hell as to how to handle his wounds nor the time to do it. Whatever attacked them was still out there in the water somewhere and the boat was going down fast.

There was damn little chance it was done with him yet too.

Tom's mind was reeling. His breaths came in ragged gasps. The pain he was in was so intense that tears rolled over the curves of his cheeks and it took effort not to black out. If he did that, Tom knew he would be dead. He needed to focus, come up with a plan. Jumping into the water seemed like a very, very bad idea but the boat was already almost under it anyway. With no other choice, Tom dove into the muddy brown surrounding the boat. The filth of it stung the wounds on his legs.

Tom lost sight of the boat, swimming for the shore as fast as his wounds would allow. Each movement he made *hurt*. By some miracle, Tom made it. Slipping and sliding, he scrambled up the muddy bank. Only when he was fully on land did Tom turn to look back. That's when he saw the top of the thing's head and eyes sticking out of the water. They glowed a hot yellow. Tom's breath caught in his throat, choking him, as his heart skipped a beat. The massive creature shot towards him. As its body rose above the surface, he saw that it was an alligator but not a normal one. The thing had to be a mutant, something horrid and sickening born from the waste that had been dumped here. Tom screamed as the mutant monster opened its mouth, seeing the rows of razor-like teeth with bits of flesh stuck amidst them.

Its powerful jaws clamped down on his midsection, his legs and lower half being swallowed whole as Tom was cut in two. His entrails, purple, red slicked strands of intestines pouring outward to uncoil in the mud. In his final seconds of life, Tom was still struggling to escape the monster. Using his hands to push what was left of his body along the ground, Tom backpedaled away leaving a trail of his own guts between himself and the giant gator. All his effort was in vain. The gator surged forward again, swallowing the rest of Tom with a single smacking snap of its jaws.

****

Burt turned up his nose at the smell of the fart Tony loosed. It was crazy foul, making Burt gag. He hurriedly rolled down the window next to him. The Ford was so old that it still took turning a handle to make it happen.

"What the hell, man?" Burt barked at Tony.

"My stomach's all torn," Tony moaned, both hands pressed over it.

"I told you not to put so much sauce on that gator meat!" Burt raged, not really feeling any sympathy for Tony's pain. "You know what mixing that crap up with drinking does to you."

"Come on, Burt," Tony begged. "That sauce was too good not to."

Burt grunted, finding that a bit hard to argue. It really was a damn good swamp sauce that had come with the gator. Feeling like the window wasn't doing enough to deal with the smell, he opened the door and slid out of the truck. The dark clouds were rolling in. It would be raining by the time the sun finished setting. He could feel it in his bones. Burt fished out a cigarette and lit up, inhaling deeply. The smoke felt warm in his lungs. He held it there before finally exhaling through his nostrils.

"You look like a damn dragon," Tony laughed and then bent over as a fresh wave of pain shot through his gut.

"Screw you," Burt shot back, giving him the finger.

He wasn't sure if Tony even saw it though. Tony had leaped from the cab of the truck and was running for the bushes, unbuckling his belt as he went. Burt shook his head in disgust.

"Stupid idiot," Burt shook his head.

The area they were parked in was right at the edge of Trenton Swamp. There were trees all around them and the road they'd driven coming in was a bumpy gravel mess. Burt worried if the rain came while they were still there, the truck was going to get stuck on the way out.

"Hurry up and get your crapping done quick, Tony," Burt shouted. "Rain's coming."

Burt leaned back into the truck, snagging the bottle of whiskey that sat in the middle of the front seat. He took a heavy chug from it and burped loudly. It was quiet other than the wet sounds of Tony's distant diarrhea that his burp seemed to echo among the trees. Burt's forehead crinkled in thought. The silence was disturbing. The normal sounds of the swamp at twilight simply weren't there. Burt felt his own stomach lurch from his sudden nervousness. His instincts told him that something was way out of whack. With another long chug, Burt emptied the remainder of the whiskey and tossed the bottle away, hopping back into the driver's seat. He closed the door, locking it, and began to roll up the window.

"Come on!" he yelled for Tony. "Get on back here!"

Still in the process of pulling up his pants, Tony came stumbling out of the trees.

"What crawled up your butt and died?" Tony was clearly feeling better now that his bowels were unloaded.

"Don't you hear it?" Burt glared at him.

"Hear what?" Tony asked, reaching the passenger side door which he had left swinging open.

"Exactly," Burt huffed.

"What the hell are you talking about?" Tony grumbled, wiping at his lips to make sure all the vomit was gone, his voice heavily slurring.

"It's too quiet," Burt explained. "There's nothing out there making a sound. Nothing. It's creepy as hell, man."

"Okay," Tony wobbled as he climbed up to take a seat inside the truck. "If you say so."

Burt rolled his eyes, wondering why he continued to have Tony as a drinking buddy.

"Close your door, man," Burt ordered. "I'm getting us out of here before that rain comes in."

"Fine," Tony slammed the door.

Cranking up the truck, Burt shifted it into reverse, putting only a little pressure on the gas. How they had parked, facing the murk of Trenton Swamp, made it difficult to turn the truck around. As he craned his head around to look back, Burt's eyes fell on the thing that was blocking the road. It was massive. Shoulders standing several feet off the ground and its body stretching to what had to be over fifteen feet in length. The thing looked like a gator but it wasn't. . .not quite. No gator could ever get as large as it was and on some areas of the scales covering its body were what appeared to be spikes. Mouth opened, the creature loosed a hiss that could be heard over the truck's engine. Its eyes, glowing in the growing darkness, burnt into Burt's soul. Seeing Burt's expression, Tony turned to look too. As soon as he saw the thing, Tony screamed like a frightened little school girl, spittle flying. His shoulder rammed into the door next to him as he fought to get it open and then went tumbling out of the truck's cab.

"Idiot!" Burt jerked around, slapping the dashboard. "What a freaking idiot!"

Tony would have been safe in the truck, at least that's what Burt was telling himself and hoping to be true. The idiot had scrambled up onto his feet and started running for the trees. Burt watched in disbelief as the massive gator thing launched itself forward, moving with a speed that seemed impossible for something its size to chase after Tony.

The huge gator got him from behind, jaws closing around the center of Tony's body. The gator's massive head shook wildly and Tony's upper half was flung in one direction while his lower half was flung in the other.

Vomit exploded up Burt's throat and out of his

mouth, splashing all over the front of his shirt, pants, and the truck's steering wheel and dashboard. Burt got it under control, stemming the eruption, as he stared in horror at the mutant gator. There was no better way to describe the creature he was looking at. With a single movement its large jaws swept up Tony's lower half from the mud and swallowed it whole.

"God have mercy," Burt mumbled, pulling on his seat belt and locking it into place. Knowing he had to do something fast or he would end up in the thing's belly too, and without enough time to really get the truck turned about to head down the gravel road he and Tony had come in on, Burt floored the gas. He used the truck as a weapon, sending it surging towards the huge gator. The crunching of metal filled his ears and the windshield in front of him shattered from the force of the impact as the truck plowed into the creature. There was a sickening crack of bone breaking. Burt didn't feel any pain though, first thinking the sound came from his own body, but it was the gator's forward right leg that had given way. The gator was making grunting noises in between high pitched almost chirping cries. It was very much still alive though which was a lot more than could be said for the truck. The Ford's front end was smashed, smoke was pouring upwards out of the motor area, and the hood was crinkled metal, folded up to the point that it kept Burt from seeing as much of the gator and its state than he liked.

Burt sat there too stunned to move, eyes bugging from their sockets. He didn't even know if he was still breathing or not. His knuckles were white from how tightly he gripped the vomit-slicked steering wheel in front of him. There were pieces of broken glass from the windshield all over him. The gator began dragging itself away from the wreck of the truck. Bright red blood leaked from where its leg was snapped. The white of bone protruded out through the scaly flesh there. The gator's movement was much slower and awkward from its injury. Still, having backed off, it now crawled around to approach the driver's side of the truck where Burt sat. His head turned slowly to the right as he saw the gator more clearly and realized what it was doing. Burt didn't want to die. He had to get away, he just had to. His fingers fumbled with the latch of his seat belt desperately trying to undo it. The belt snapped loose and Burt threw himself across the truck's cab. He kept a .38 revolver in the glove box. Retrieving the weapon, Burt kicked at the passenger side door. It wasn't fully closed and it flung wide open. Burt tumbled through it, out of the truck's cab, landing on his hands and knees with a grunt. Lightning flashed in the black clouds gathering over the swamp. At that moment, the alligator struck the truck. The vehicle was lifted up on the driver's side from the impact with another crunch of metal before flopping back onto the ground. Panic grew in Burt as he scrambled to his feet and jumped away from the truck.

The huge alligator hissed, dragging itself around the vehicle. Its eyes were locked on him as Burt looked around to see it coming his way. Something clicked inside of Burt like someone flicking a switch. His fear turned into anger on the drop of a dime. This freaking thing had killed his friend, trashed his truck, and was coming to make him into an early evening meal. It was too much, way too much. Burt stood his ground, shifting into a two handed firing position, bringing up the .38.

"Okay, you big bastard," Burt snarled. "It's your turn to get some."

The .38 boomed as Burt squeezed its trigger. He aimed for the center of the gator's head, hoping to put a round straight into its brain. The bullet struck the gator's scales, sparking as it hit, and bounced harmlessly away.

"Damn it!" Burt wailed. His .38 boomed in rapid succession. The massive alligator kept coming towards him, each of his shots unable to penetrate its scales and the thickness of its skull.

The .38 clicked empty. Eyes bugging, Burt stared at the gator in disbelief that he hadn't managed to hurt it at all. There were no extra bullets to reload with. Throwing the .38 at the alligator, he spun to flee its hissing wrath only to trip over his own feet. Burt went down hard. . . and then the gator was on him. His head came around to look directly into its wide open mouth. The gator's powerful jaws came together on Burt's head, crushing it like an over ripe melon. Blood and brain matter exploded out from the edges of the gator's mouth. His headless body flopped over and lay there twitching in front.

The gator ripped and tore at Burt's body, eating its fill of his flesh and entrails before dragging itself into the murky waters of Trenton Swamp, vanishing beneath them.

****

Sheriff Peterson sat behind his desk with his booted feet propped on top of it. His swivel chair squeaked as he rocked ever so slightly in it. Mary hadn't been happy when he'd called to say that he wasn't even sure making it home tonight was possible. He had one hell of a mess to deal with. Thankfully, at least for now, the national guard was letting him handle things. Having seen that their boys had been lost to what was clearly some sort of animal and not a terrorist attack or a soldier going off the deep end on a psychotic killing spree, they had backed off. The problem was figuring out what in the hell sort of animal could kill four trained and armed soldiers? There were damn big and violent gators in Trenton Swamp for sure. The things could sneak up on you in those murky waters and end you before you even knew they were there. Still, one gator versus four armed men, it didn't make sense. Apex predator or not, that was just too much. And then there were the prints they had been able to retrieve from the shore. They were screwy as hell. He'd lived here long enough to know a gator print when he saw it. That's what these prints looked like too except that they were way the hell too big. Sheriff Peterson was slowly coming around to accept that his deputy Zack's theory that they were dealing with a freaking monster might just be the best theory they had. Dealing with monsters wasn't something that was in the normal playbook.

There was a knock on the door of his office.

"Come on in," Sheriff Peterson called out. "Especially if you're bringing some coffee with you."

Stacia, his lead deputy, entered and shut the door

behind her. From the expression on her face he knew that whatever she was about to tell him wasn't going to make things any easier.

"No luck on the coffee but I've got reports back from all usuals," Stacia said.

"Do tell," Sheriff Peterson frowned.

"The prints came back as gator or rather that's what they are closest to being just like you thought they would," Stacia shook her head. "But they are slightly off and certainly much larger than they should be."

"We already pretty much knew that without the opinion of some wildlife guy," Sheriff Peterson swung his feet from the desk. His boots thudded heavily onto the floor as he shifted in his chair to sit up straight.

"Yeah," Stacia agreed.

"What else?" Sheriff Peterson asked.

"The same from the coroner," Stacia said. "The teeth marks on the body match those of a gator other than their size as well."

"Phew," Sheriff Peterson leaned forward, steepling his fingers in front of his lips. "Ain't nothing right about any of this."

"Nope," Stacia agreed again. "You figured out what we're doing about it yet?"

"Working on it," he grinned up at her. "You got

any ideas?"

Sheriff Peterson liked to include his better deputies in the working of the department, knowing that he wasn't going to be around forever and the more they learned the part things would continue after he was gone. And Stacia was flat out the best of his people. She'd well earned her spot as lead deputy. Tough, smart as hell, level headed, and gifted with keen instincts, deputies just didn't come any better. Stacia had been a Godsend from the second he hired her. With her at the department's helm, Sheriff Peterson could take a day off and not worry about everything in town collapsing into the depths of hell and chaos.

"Before we get into talking about that, I've got some more news you're not going to like," Stacia said.

"Hit me with it," Sheriff Peterson ordered.

Stacia told him exactly what he expected to hear, "There's been another attack."

"Figured," Sheriff Peterson sighed. "Where?"

"Edge of Trenton Swamp, south of town," she answered.

"How many?" he eyed her, hoping the number was low.

"Two," Stacia held up the pointer and middle fingers of her right hand. "Our resident troublemakers, Burt and Tony. Looks like the two of them were out for an evening of drinking, as usual, and things took a bad turn."

Sheriff Peterson grunted. "Almost feel bad for that big gator. Those two couldn't have gone down well. They would make just about anything sick."

Stacia stared at him, reminding Sheriff Peterson that his humor wasn't always funny or even appropriate at times.

"Yeah, I know," Sheriff Peterson shrugged. "I'll keep working on it. Still, as far as victims go, it could have been a lot worse. Imagine if some kids had been out there playing."

Ignoring that last bit, Stacia opened the file she'd brought with her and passed him a photo from it. The shot was of Burt's truck.

"Holy. . ." Sheriff Peterson exclaimed, seeing the amount of damage done to the vehicle in the picture. "Just how the hell big is this gator?"

"Best guess?" Stacia asked.

"I got my own guess but go ahead," he urged her.

"Based on the prints, the damage to the truck, etc.," Stacia wore a freaked out expression, "We're guessing this gator is at least eighteen feet long with a shoulder height of four feet or more."

Sheriff Peterson whistled. "That's a damn big gator. Makes sense though from the looks of Burt's truck. Those good ole boys never had a chance."

Stacia shook her head in agreement. "Burt did get off some shots with a .38. No indication that they did squat to the gator and they sure didn't save him."

"This thing must be as armored as it is large." Sheriff Peterson got up from his chair, walking to the window behind where he had been sitting. "That ain't good."

"Explains how the guardsmen it ate failed to stop it," Stacia pointed out.

"That it does," Sheriff Peterson clasped his hands behind his back, looking out and up at the night sky through the window. "I ain't looking forward to running into a gator with scales tough enough to stand up to M16 fire."

"Me either," Stacia frowned. "Now about that. . ."

"We're not calling the Guard to help, not yet," Sheriff Peterson told her. "Things are gonna be tricky enough as it is without those overconfident, weekend warriors stomping around out there."

"Fair," Stacia said. "I can't argue that. I don't know how long we'll be able to keep them out of it though once this new killing hits the press."

"Who else knows about Burt and Tony?" Sheriff Peterson turned to face her.

"Just the kids who were headed out there to get it on and instead got the crap scared out of them, the ambulance crews, and our people."

"Well let's make sure those kids don't say a thing to anyone they don't have to," Sheriff Peterson ordered.

"We've still got them here at the station finishing up their statements so that's do-able," Stacia assured him.

"Good," Sheriff Peterson was glad for any break he could catch.

"If we're not calling in the Guard. . ." Stacia started.

"We'll be calling in the State guys," Sheriff Peterson said. "Talk to Captain Hightower and see how many officers he can spare for tomorrow."

"Tomorrow, huh?" Stacia asked.

Sheriff Peterson nodded. "I want us all out there at the crack of dawn. We need to get this thing before it eats anyone else or worse, decides to get curious and pays a visit to town. I'm gonna need to call in the Green Brothers and the Suttons too."

"Both of them?" Stacia cocked an eyebrow.

The Green Brothers and the Suttons were the two best gator hunting operations in this part of the state. They both kicked butt at what they did. The only issue was there was a fierce competition between them. The families hated each other as much as the Capulets and Montagues. Their feud was famous and more than once he and his deputies had been called out to keep one side or the other from getting killed.

"Both of them," Sheriff Peterson repeated firmly.

"God help us," Stacia rolled her eyes. "You sure you don't want to call in the Guard instead?"

"We need the best," Sheriff Peterson shrugged, "and all the help we can get. With both of them on the job, it increases our shot of catching this thing before it does eat some poor kids dumb enough to go out into the swamp by themselves."

Stacia had started out of his office but paused in the doorway looking back at him a final time, "Anything else?"

"Yeah, call in all our people too," Sheriff Peterson returned to his chair. "I want patrols on the southern side of town doubled, tripled if possible, for the rest of the night. Make sure our people know what they're keeping an eye out for too."

"Will do," Stacia said. "I'm on it."

Sheriff Peterson watched her go, knowing full well how capable Stacia was and she would have it all done and everyone gathered together before the sun rose. Wishing he was home with Mary, he sighed, and slumped forward onto his desk, lowering his head onto his arms. His age and exhaustion were catching up with him. Part of him wondered if it might be worth it to run home for just a few hours, get a hug, a kiss, and a nap, but Sheriff Peterson knew that wasn't a viable idea. He needed to be here in case their monster gator struck again.

****

Gary glanced at the clock next to his bed. Its screen read 4:30. He chuckled at seeing that exact time. It made him remember an old song by the Spin Doctors. Falling asleep was far easier than he'd thought it would be but now he was awake in the wee hours and knew that he was up to stay. There was no hope of getting his mind to shut down again.

Rolling out of bed, his feet thudded onto the floor. The day was already warm. It would likely be blistering hot by midday. Gary headed straight for a shower and shave then got dressed. Dressed in a comfortable black t-shirt and jeans, Gary realized that there was no food in the house. He hadn't made a grocery run yet. That seemed like it would be a lot more fun than working on getting the new place in order anyway plus making the run to get them gave him an excuse to check out the closest town. He'd passed through it on the way in but hadn't really paid attention.

Bentonville, that was the town's name, he recalled, walking out onto the small front porch and taking in a breath of fresh, morning air. The sun wasn't up yet and everything was wet. It had rained overnight. Gary turned his head in the direction of the distant swamp. You could see the edge of it, if only barely, from his house. Gary wasn't sure how he felt about the swamp. Exploring it held no interest for him. The trio of houses between his and Trenton Swamp though did. All of them were small but still larger than his own. He'd need to check them out, find out who his neighbors were, and if there were going to be issues with them. If any of them had come over yesterday to welcome him, he'd been asleep with the door locked and hadn't heard them.

Gary gnawed at the skin below the tip of his thumb nail on his right hand. Dealing with people wasn't something he was great at. Oh, he could get by but that didn't mean he liked it. His neighbors all looked to be home but it was far too early to walk down the road and say hello to any of them. It would have to be done sooner or later and there was no getting around it. He didn't want to appear like some kind of reclusive weirdo. That simply wouldn't do. It wasn't as if there was anyone hunting for him but there was also no point in taking chances. In the course of his career, Gary knew very well that he had made a lot of enemies, most of them were dead but not all. He doubted the FBI and CIA were going to waste resources coming after him. As long as he stayed under the radar and inactive, everything should be just fine.

This truly was going to be good for him, taking a break, living out here. If and when he returned to his work, Gary knew that things would be different and that was a good thing. But then, he might never go back. Even with all that Eva took from him, there was enough in his secret, emergency accounts to give him time enough to find a new line of work. Part of him, somewhere deep down, missed her. Waking up alone didn't bring that home to him as much as standing out here in the dark looking up at the morning sky. He supposed it was the rain that brought her to mind. She loved it so much. He could almost taste her lips on his, feel the smoothness and softness of her skin on his palms, and smell her hair. Gary grunted, chasing the memories and feelings away. Emotions were always the enemy. They just were and he didn't care for them.

Bentonville was only about ten minutes away and it was so very early. Nonetheless, Gary was eager to get going. He started down the steps from the porch and froze. A feeling came over him, one that set him on edge. Gary couldn't identify what it was or figure out where it came from, but his gut was telling him not to go into town without being ready for anything that might come at him there. What the hell that could be was just as much of a mystery. He knew better than to not trust his instincts, however, and headed back into the house, grabbing one of his duffel bags. He tossed it into his car from the passenger side and went around to slide into the driver's seat. Cranking up, Gary backed out onto the road, swinging the car around in the direction of Bentonville.

Clicking on the radio, a news report caught his attention as he was scrolling through the channels. He paused on it, listening intently. The report was about a missing reporter who was supposedly working on a story about a big corporation local to the area. The guy telling it all was playing it off as if there might be more to the reporter's disappearance than just getting lost in the swamp. Drama, Gary sighed, it apparently followed him everywhere. As strange and off putting as the news was, it didn't have crap to do with him, Gary reminded himself of that. The only thing that should be mattering to him right now was where in the hell he could get a cup of hot, black coffee. Flipping the radio dial, he settled on a station playing classic rock and tried to lose himself in the music.

The road from his house to Bentonville was smooth sailing. He passed very little traffic. It was a Saturday so Gary figured most people were in bed enjoying the weekend. The drive went by fast. Before he knew it, Gary had hit the main street that ran through the center of the small town of Bentonville. As he came to a stop at the first red light in the town, Gary looked around at the little mom and pop stores that lined the street. It was all so quiet and quaint.

Up ahead, Gary saw lights coming on in the diner at the end of the street. He headed straight for it, pulling into its lot. The place was shaped like a trailer, long and not overly wide. Through its windows, he saw that it had a fifties style vibe. The lot was empty around him other than a beat up Toyota parked at the edge of the lot bordering the trees on its western side. There didn't appear to be any other patrons than himself. The Toyota surely belonged to the young woman flitting about in the diner, getting it ready to open. She was somewhere in her early twenties by his best guess, thin, with angular features, and long, jet black hair, cinched back tightly in a pony tail. Her uniform was a cliche red and white that made Gary think of a cheap, paper napkin.

The sign on the door hadn't been flipped and still read closed. Gary ignored it, getting out, and walking up the small set of steps to the diner's main door. It was glass and the young waitress looked over at him, startled, as his knuckles rapped against it. Her expression quickly switched from surprise to that of frustrated, mild anger.

“We're closed!” she yelled at him through the glass door.

Gary, his voice raised, hoping she would be able to hear him, responded, “I'm new in town. Just bought a place out near Trenton Swamp. All I want is some coffee. Can you help me out?”

The young waitress rolled her eyes but hurried over to the door.

“How do I know you're not planning on robbing the place or something worse?” she challenged him. Gary couldn't quite tell if she was joking or not.

He shrugged, fishing out his wallet. Pressing his driver's license against the glass of the door so that she could see it, he said, “I'm Gary Brander, just a guy dying of caffeine withdrawal.”

The young waitress smirked and began to fumble with the lock. Swinging the door inward, she said, “Guess I'm a big softie because I believe you.”

“Thank you,” Gary flashed a grin.

Sauntering up to the counter, he took a seat on

one of the stools at it.

"Let me finish up wiping the tables and I'll get some coffee going," the young waitress told him.

"Leaving me hanging already, huh?" Gary teased her. "I didn't catch your name."

"Shel," she answered, not bothering to look his way, intently focused on her cleaning.

"That short for Shelly?" Gary asked.

Shel turned, hands on hips, scowling at him. "For a person supposedly in desperate need of coffee, you seem rather awake and on it."

"Just because I'm able to be a bit witty without coffee doesn't mean I enjoy it," Gary shot back.

"Witty? Is that what we're calling it?" Shel chuckled.

Gary watched as she hurried on around the counter and got the coffee going. The smell of it was heavenly.

"So you're new to Bentonville, huh?" Shel leaned over the counter.

"Yeah," Gary nodded. "Just got in yesterday. Haven't even unpacked yet."

"So you're what, just taking in the sights? We don't get many tourists around these parts," Shel frowned.

"No," Gary stared at the dark liquid she was now pouring into a mug for him. She noticed.

Smirking, Shel sat the mug in front of him. “Want me to put some ice in it so you can drink it faster?”

Gary laughed. “I'll manage.”

“So you're not a tourist then, huh?” Shel smiled.

“I bought a house down near Trenton Swamp,” Gary told her.

“Bet you got it cheap,” Shel shook her head.

“Something I should know?” Gary asked, taking a sip of the coffee she'd made for him.

“That's not a great area down that way.” Shel flipped some rogue strands of her black hair from her face.

“Gang violence?” Gary gave her his own smirk.

“I can see that coffee is already doing you some good,” she quipped.

“Then what's the deal?” Gary pressed.

“I've heard a lot of folks go missing in that swamp,” Shel waved a hand dismissively. “I sure wouldn't want to live near it.”

“I can take care of myself,” Gary said matter-of-factly.

“I pegged you as a military guy,” Shel admitted. “That's why I let you in before we're really open.”

“You're right,” Gary nodded. “I did my time.”

“You don't have to talk about it,” Shel frowned as if sensing he didn't want to.

"Thanks," Gary took another sip of his coffee.

It was obvious she had been hoping for more in terms of a response. Gary had nothing he was willing to share though.

The door to the diner swung open and a trio of elderly gentlemen entered. They were carrying on among themselves. Shel's expression let him know at once that they were regulars.

"Morning, boys!" she called out to them.

"Morning, Shel," the shortest of them with the longest gray beard greeted her.

"Well, it looks like we're open now," Shel frowned.

A few minutes earlier, Gary had noticed that the lights in the kitchen had come on. The diner's cook had to have arrived and was getting ready for his or her day in the back.

Shel hurried away to wait on the old men who took a booth far away from where he sat at the counter. Gary sipped at his coffee and waited patiently on her to come back so that he could get a refill.

****

A convoy of vehicles drove along the road from Bentonville to Trenton Swamp. Gary had missed seeing them by mere minutes. In the lead car,

Deputy Stacia was at the wheel with Sheriff Peterson next to her in the passenger's seat. Behind them were several more cars with flashing siren lights, both from their department and those belonging to state troopers. Accompanying them were a few trucks, two of them hauling boats on trailers. Those were the Suttons and the Green Brothers.

"You sure about this?" Stacia asked, glancing over at him.

Sheriff Peterson was stretched out comfortably, gripping a cup of steaming, black coffee. "Hell Stacia, I got nothing else. We need to find and kill that giant monster out there and that's all there is to it."

"With the Green Brothers and Suttons along, I'd say the odds of us finding the thing are at least in our favor," Stacia commented.

"Yep," Sheriff Peterson agreed. "The additional manpower from the state boys will help with that too. Besides, something as big as this thing seems to be, how hard could it be to find anyway?"

"I guess we'll see," Stacia didn't fully agree with the last bit. Even if the gator was as big as they thought it was likely to be didn't mean it wasn't cunning and dang good at hiding. The thing had to be or surely it would have been spotted by someone a long time ago.

The cars all headed down a side road that led to a place where the gator hunters could put their boats into the water. It was as good a spot as any to set up a makeshift base camp too. From there, the plan was for his people and the state troopers to set out on foot through the swamp while the gator hunters came at it from the water side of things.

The trucks, with their trailers and boats, kept going as the road led into a large, open area. The rest of the convoy came to a stop though, officers spilling out of their cars.

Captain Hightower wasn't with the troopers he'd sent. Sheriff Peterson didn't give a damn. He was just glad to have the extra manpower. The extra four men were more eyes and guns that could be brought to bear in the search for the giant gator.

Stacia was already out of their car. He got out too, glancing across to see her chambering a round in the shotgun she held.

"What?" she asked, catching his look. "You know I like to be prepared."

Sheriff Peterson couldn't stop the lopsided grin that spread his lips. "Yeah, I know you do."

"Hopefully those hunter people will drive that gator onto land, straight to us," Stacia said.

Shaking his head, he countered that with,

"Personally I hope they kill the damn thing out there in the water and just bring back its corpse."

"Where's your sense of adventure?" Stacia chided him.

With a sigh, he reached into the car and picked up his Barrett M82.

Stacia made a face. "Just have to show me up, huh?"

He knew she meant how the extremely powerful rifle compared to her shotgun.

Shrugging, he started towards the swamp. "Let's get going already. Maybe with a bit of luck, I can actually make it home in time for dinner tonight."

Angry yells and shouts coming from where the hunters' boats were being put into the water stopped him though. Sheriff Peterson saw the Suttons and the Green Brothers crews about to come to blow and knew he was going to have to break it up. He motioned for Stacia to come along as backup as he walked towards the boat. The Suttons' was already in the water while the Green Brothers' was still on the shore waiting to be put in.

Rita Sutton was in the boat, just off the shore. She was yelling too. She was the mother figure and leader of the Sutton clan. The string of swear words spilling from her mouth would have made the most jaded sailor blush.

The other Suttons present, Tristan and Luka, between the Green Brothers group and the water. The Green Brothers were represented by both of the brothers, Graham and Edward themselves, along with Graham's wife, Emily. They were screaming right back at the Suttons. It was Emily that caught Sheriff Peterson's attention. The little woman just looked so out of place as a gator hunter. She stood around five foot five and was rail thin. Her legs though were long for her body and her butt cheeks super firm and tight through the daisy duke shorts she wore. Rather disgusted with himself for staring longer than he should at her rump before looking up to Emily's almost snarling face, Sheriff Peterson hoped that Stacia hadn't noticed his indiscretion.

“Hey!” he shouted, drawing the attention of the Suttons and the Green Brothers crew both. “What the hell is going on?”

“Those bastards cut us off and. . .” Emily raged. The deepness of her voice from such a lithe and little body always shocked him. There was a gravelness to it as well that somehow was just as sexy as her lower half. Not that her upper half was bad. Emily's features were angular and sharp, her hair long and light brown, and skin well tanned. Her breasts were small, sure, but what they lacked in size, they made up for in perkiness.

Sheriff Peterson raised a hand to silence her.

"It doesn't damn well matter who gets in the water first now, does it?" he challenged the Green Brothers crew.

"But. . ." Edward Green took a step towards him.

"Enough!" Sheriff Peterson bellowed. "You people just need to stay the hell out of each other's way out there on the water and bring me that freaking gator that's eating folks around here."

Gesturing at the two Suttons on the shore to join Rita in their boat, he said, "Get on out there. Now!"

Tristan and Luke didn't need to be told twice. They splashed out, wading their way to the boat. As soon as they were aboard, Rita flipped both him and the other crew of gator hunters off and poured power to its engine. The trio of them sped away from the shore. Sheriff Peterson was struck by the sharp contrast of the two women. Rita was as chubby as Emily was thin. She was a decade older too and her breasts were beginning to change with age. Her thighs were massive, threatening to tear through the ragged jeans she wore. Rita's expression was a perpetual scowl even during her best moments. And her hair was thick and bleached blonde adding to her punk appearance. It was hard not to automatically take Emily's side but that was part of the job, to remain neutral in their conflict, and make sure the real job got done. That big gator had to be found and destroyed.

"Sheriff," Emily said to him, "That wasn't right. We should have been the first ones in but you just wait, we will be the first ones back and with your big gator too."

"I sure as hell hope so," he told Emily.

He and Stacia didn't stick around to watch the Green Brothers' crew get their boat in. They headed on into the swamp with one of the state troopers named Cooper joining them. Sheriff Peterson's other deputies along with the other troopers had all already entered the swamp and were spreading out in various directions to search for the gator.

Meanwhile, out on the open water, the Suttons were getting to work at doing their thing. Normally shooting a gator before it was snagged and brought under control was illegal. That wasn't the case today. Sheriff Peterson had cleared them to do just about anything they needed to in order to bag the killer gator that was rampaging through Trenton Swamp. Tristan had finished setting up the usual bait lines with chunks of meat dangling over the water. He settled in taking a seat across from Luka. Reaching down, Tristan picked up his gator killer shotgun. The thing was an almost laughable attempt at overkill firepower. He'd made the thing himself.

The shotgun had three barrels, not two, with all of them in a strangely shaped, tri-gun formation. It looked likely to blow up in your face when the triggers were squeezed but Tristan was good with guns and despite its appearance, the tri-barrel shotgun would hold up and get the job done.

Luka was armed with a .308 Winchester rifle. It was a bolt action weapon and not meant for rapid fire but between its high powered, long range scope and large caliber rounds, one shot was usually enough to blow the hell out of whatever you were shooting at. Both Tristan and Luka also wore sidearms. Sticking with his love for wanton overkill, there was a Diablo, double barrel, 12 gauge, shotgun pistol holstered on his right hip. For all its stopping power though, the Diablo's range was extremely limited. It was meant as a last defense. Luka, not so obsessed with things going boom as Tristan, had a standard Glock 43 on his hip. The thing was next to useless against gators unless your shots were super precise and spot on. Luka was a heck of a marksman but even so, Rita and Tristan always gave him hell about the lameness of his pistol. When they did, Luka would argue that there were more dangers in the swamps than just gators. Rita carried no sidearm but there was a pump action shotgun propped beside her where she sat at the boat's motor, guiding it across the small lake.

“Them bastards. . .” Rita was still muttering about the Green Brothers crew. “Them damn, smug bastards.”

“Ah Mom,” Tristan shook his head. “Forget about it. You don't need to be hanging onto negativity like that. It ain't good for you.”

Tristan's left hand stroked at his long, red beard.

“Don't you come at me with that self-help crap! You know I don't care for it,” Rita snapped.

“He's just worried about you,” Luka chimed in. “The doctor said that you. . .”

“Did I ask you to remind me of what that quack said?” Rita's head jerked around as she turned to glare at Luka.

“No ma'am,” he answered. “You did not.”

“Damn right I didn't,” Rita spat.

Their boat had a mini-sonar tracker and its screen was positioned just below where Rita sat so that she could easily keep an eye on it. Noticing movement on it, she bit her lip, took a breath to bring her anger under control, and said, “Boys, we got ourselves some company coming.”

The Suttons truly were among the best gator hunters around. They had years of experience hunting and killing the animals. When Sheriff

Peterson told them about the size of the gator they were after today, none of them believed him. They knew that eye witness accounts could be distorted and screwed up, things exaggerated out of proportion. Rita laughed out loud and told the sheriff just how full of it he had to be. . . that was until shown the casts of the gator's prints and pictures of the four national guardsmen that the beast had made a meal out of. Those casts and pics scared the hell out of the Green Brothers so that was something. Rita wasn't oblivious to how dangerous one the size of the thing out here could be but to her it wasn't so much horrifying as simply worrisome. A little extra caution dealing with the monster and they would be fine. Seeing the size of the creature that was moving beneath the water and coming toward them now though, Rita began to sweat more than she already was from the heat of the day.

"Watch it now," Rita warned, "The gator is. . ."

Rita never got out the rest of her words. The gator's speed increased and it slammed into their boat with such force it was nearly flipped over. The side caved inward, metal bending and wood splintering.

"Holy!" Tristan cried out, as he was nearly flung over the side.

Luka was holding on for dear life too. A shard of

wood had embedded itself in his left leg. Hyped up on sudden adrenaline, Luka grabbed it, yanking the wood out. Blood splattered onto the floor of the boat at his feet.

Rita fought to get the boat under control as it was knocked off course by the impact. She had unintentionally increased its speed and didn't want it flipping over from how hard it was bouncing across the water. Rita won the fight, stabilizing the boat.

“What the hell hit us?” Luka shouted. “Ain't no way in hell that was a gator!”

“Yeah it was, boy!” Rita snapped. “It was a freaking giant one. Haven't you been paying attention to what we're out here after?”

“I see it!” Tristan yelled, pointing.

Rita's head craned around to look behind the speeding boat. . . and there it was. The gator was like something from the depths of hell. She would have not believed something like it could even exist. In all her years of gator hunting, she had never heard of a gator of its size. Rita's bladder almost emptied itself but she managed not to pee her pants. She was scared. . .scared as hell. The gator was gaining on the boat. Its eyes glowed a hellish red, full of primal rage and fury.

The side of the boat was caved inward where the gator had struck it. The metal was buckling and the wood a broken mess. They were taking on some water but weren't in danger of sinking.

Tristan, recovered and back on his game, stood up, taking aim at the quickly approaching gator with his tri-barrel shotgun. His head gave a slight, frustrated shake as Tristan realized the gator wasn't just out of range but the water was screwing up any shot he took at it too. There just wasn't enough of the gator's head for him to even try to hit at such a distance.

“Sit your arse down!” Rita barked.

The motor suddenly squealed and cut out.

“Damn it!” Rita struggled to see what had happened.

The gator shot forward like a streak of lightning, its head sinking beneath the surface. It slammed into the motor boat from beneath it. The boat was thrown upwards. Rita, Tristan, and Luka were all flung into the air and came back down splashing into the water. Rita died first. The gator swept in, jaws closing on Rita. The water churned red where it took her under.

“Mum!” Tristan screamed. He managed to keep hold of his shotgun as he was tossed from the boat. Clutching it tightly, knuckles white, Tristan could only wait for the gator to come up again.

Nearby, Luka was straining to keep himself

afloat. His injured leg made the doggie paddling he was doing to keep his head above the surface difficult.

"She's dead, man!" Luka shouted. "And that thing is coming for us next!"

Tristan saw that Luka had lost his rifle but had managed to draw his Glock. Not that it would do him any good. The 9mm weapon was questionable at best against a normal gator, much less this thing that was coming for them.

"We gotta get to the shore!" Luka warned.

That was hopeless and Tristan knew it. The gator was a hell of a lot faster than they were. It could take them both out before either of them reached the distant muddy banks at the edge of the swamp. He wasn't even going to try for it. His best chance was to wait on the gator to come at him and blow its freaking face off. At point blank, his tri-barrel shotgun would wreck the bastard. He had faith that it would anyway.

The water around Tristan and Luka had become eerily calm. Several bits of Rita had broken the surface and were floating, bobbing up and down. Bile rose up in Tristan's throat. He forced it down, swallowing hard to keep from vomiting.

"Look out!" Tristan heard Luka yell. He twisted his body around in the water to see the massive gator. With the speed of a torpedo the thing was plowing directly at him. Tristan tried to bring his shotgun level with the gator but it went by him in a blur. Stunned, he stared after the massive creature in shock. The thing hadn't been after him at all. It was going for Luka. The Glock in his brother's hands cracked in rapid succession. The 9mm rounds sparked harmlessly off the gator's thick, armor-like scales and then Luka shrieked in pain. His cry became a sickening gargle as Luka disappeared into the water.

"God help me, God help me, God help me," Tristan repeated over and over, trying to steady himself. There was no question that Luka was dead. The amount of red that rose up, spreading out over the surface above where he'd been dragged down made that much obvious.

His hands shaking, Tristan held his tri-barrel shotgun ready, waiting for the gator to surface again and come at him next. His breaths were ragged gasps as he sucked in one after another. Tristan's heart was pounding so hard inside his chest it felt like it was hammering against his ribs.

Seconds ticked by like hours. His head jerked about this way and that, eyes scanning for any sign of the gator. He couldn't see it at all. The water was still and calm. After a couple of minutes had passed,

Tristan realized that the gator was gone. Why, he had no idea. Maybe the thing had eaten its fill with Rita and Luka. Maybe its collisions with their boat had hurt it somehow. It didn't really matter. All that mattered was that the huge thing seemed to not be around anymore.

Tristan sprang into motion, swimming like hell for the muddy banks at the edge of the swamp.

****

Edward, Graham, and Emily Green's boat bounced over the open water. Graham was piloting it. Edward sat near its bow, holding a high powered hunting rifle. Emily was between them in the center of the boat, using the boat's sonar gear to keep an eye out for any sign of gators below the surface.

"Hey!" Edward shouted. "Slow us down!"

Graham lowered the power to the engine, reducing the boat's speed.

"Do you see that?" Edward pointed up ahead of them at something metallic and gleaming in the sunlight.

Graham directed their boat cautiously in the direction of the object.

"Frag me," Edward muttered. "That's. . ."

"The Suttons' boat," Emily finished for him.

"Yeesh," Edward was shaking his head.

“Something knocked the hell out of it,” Emily pointed at a large dent in the now upturned lower hull of the boat.

“You don't think. . .” Emily frowned.

“Sure as hell,” Graham chimed in from where he sat. “I'd stake my life that the giant gator we're out here after did that.”

“Oh God,” Emily suddenly exclaimed as she saw the body parts floating near the boat. She leaned over the edge of their boat, vomiting up her breakfast.

“That's Rita's arm,” Edward said to no one in particular, trying not to be sick too.

“Looks like that gator the sheriff told us about made a bloody meal out of them,” Graham said.

“Doesn't bode too well, does it?” Edward commented.

“The Suttons were idiots,” Graham grunted. “We're not.”

Graham looked at Emily, “Anything out there?”

She had recovered enough to take a look at the sonar screen and shake her head.

“What you thinking?” Edward asked.

“That going after this thing out here is a mistake,” Graham eyed the water around the boat. “It's too risky.”

“Ya think?” Emily quipped.

"I'm taking us back," Graham told them and revved the boat's engine, bringing it around.

"I'm thinking we're gonna need some bigger guns," Edward said, his tone not humorous at all.

"We'll get them," Graham assured him.

By the time they reached the point where they'd put the boat in the water, the makeshift base camp for the entire operation was pretty much cleared out. Everyone was already off in the swamp, trudging through its mud and murk, searching for the giant gator on foot.

Deputy Nations from Sheriff Peterson's department, a thin, pale guy with nerdy glasses, saw them come and begin hauling their boat onto the shore. He strolled over with an official air to ask, "What are you people doing back already?"

"The Suttons are dead," Graham answered. "Your sheriff's big gator wrecked their boat and ate them."

Nations blinked and then stared at the Green Brothers crew clearly not having a clue how to respond to what he had just been told.

"It's too dangerous out there on the water in the boat the size of the one we brought," Emily explained. "We're back to switch our gear and join the search on foot in the swamp."

"I'll be damned," Nations shook his head. "The

Suttons are really dead? All of them?"

"From what we could see, yeah," Edward thumped the deputy on his shoulder. "That gator ain't screwing around."

"I'll let the sheriff know about them," Nations said and hurried off.

"Think we just scared him to death," Emily said.

"Hell, I'm scared to death," Edward huffed.

"Enough," Graham's voice was firm and hard. "Don't be letting what happened to the Suttons get to you. We still got a job to do and I need both of your heads in the game."

The trio finished getting their boat secured and then went to work trading out gear. All of them donned heavy, protective pants despite the heat. Edward took an AK-47 out of the truck. Its magazine was loaded up with armor piercing rounds. If the sheriff questioned him about it, Edward was going to have to do some fast thinking. Thankfully, Sheriff Peterson, from what he had seen, was fully focused on the giant gator and nothing else. Edward also strapped a snub nose .38 to the side of his boot.

Graham opted to carry a pump action 12 gauge with him though he did add a .44 Magnum as his sidearm. Glancing over at Emily, he saw she wasn't screwing around either. His cute, little wife had picked up a breach loading but very powerful, double barreled shotgun. She shoved a handful of extra shells into a pocket and, noticing him watching, flashed Graham a smile.

They made one heck of a team, out hunting for gators, as business partners, in the bed. . . Graham knew he was as blessed as any man could be. Though like any humans, they fought from time to time and didn't always see eye to eye, a man couldn't ask for a better wife than Emily. He felt like whistling at how sexy she was but didn't. They all needed to focus just like he had told them that they did.

Deputy Nations came hurrying back in their direction.

"Hey!" he called out, "hold up!"

"What ya need, Deputy?" Edward asked before Graham could.

"Sheriff Peterson says I need to go in with y'all," Deputy Nations answered.

"I don't think that's a good idea," Emily frowned.

Edward nodded, backing her up, "We work alone, Nations. Having you with us will only slow us down."

"Sorry," Deputy Nations told them, "My hands are tied, folks. Gotta do what the sheriff tells me to."

“Fine,” Graham huffed. “Just try to keep up and stay out of the way.”

“Yeah,” Edward moved to lay a hand on the deputy's shoulder, “And just listen to what we tell you. We wouldn't want you becoming gator food now, would we?”

Looking suddenly pale, Deputy Nations said, “Copy that.”

The Green Brothers crew, with its added member, set out into the swamp at a cautious but slightly hurried pace.

****

Tristan couldn't believe that he was alive. He held his tri-barrel shotgun tightly with one hand while his other patted over his upper body, pounding it, to make sure he was really intact and not dreaming. When Tristan realized that he was really okay, he exhaled a long, slow breath.

He stood in the mud at the edge of the bank where the swamp met the open water beyond it. There was no sign of the boat or of Rita and Luka. Tristan didn't know how long he'd been out. After reaching the bank, as soon as he had scrambled out of the water, the shock of it all had knocked him out. Passing out like a school kid or some city slicker made Tristan really ticked with himself but it had happened nonetheless. . . awake again now, Tristan had no idea where he was. There wasn't exactly a raging current to the water but you could drift on it like on any body of water. That had to be what happened to the wreckage of the boat. That was his best guess at any rate.

His mind didn't want to accept that Rita and Luka were dead. They were though. He had watched them die. A shiver ran through him and goosebumps grew on his sweat slicked and mud smeared skin. He was alone out here with no way to call for help. His cell was gone. He had lost it somehow in the struggle to stay alive and not get eaten by the abomination out there in the water. And the radio had been on the boat.

The swamp was quiet behind him and there was no sign of the giant alligator in the water. The sun hadn't quite reached its zenith in the sky. The air was stifling, humid and hot beneath its burning rays. Tristan turned and trudged into the swamp. The terrain was parts standing water, parts firm, solid ground, and mostly mud. The path ahead shifted between the three as Tristan kept moving; one minute he was wading, watching out for sharp drop offs, and the next struggling not to get stuck in mud to the point of losing his boots.

A loud, sharp hiss from off the path somewhere

made Tristan freeze in his tracks and nearly pee his pants. Afraid to move, he cut his eyes one way then the other, trying to get a look at whatever made the hissing noise. A whimper escaped his clinched lips as Tristan saw the gator. It was several yards away, blended into the grays and browns of the swamp, among a patch of trees, some dead and decaying where they stood in ankle deep water. The gator's eyes were bright yellow and unblinking. Tristan shifted his gaze away from them not wanting to make the monster angry by engaging it in a staring contest. His heart was pounding in his chest, throat closing up with fear. Tristan's knuckles went white from how tightly his grip on the tri-barrel shotgun in his hands became. He didn't dare move. It was scary to even breathe. Tristan didn't want to do anything to upset the giant alligator and make it come for him.

Tristan stood like a statue, hoping and praying the alligator would lose interest in staring at him and move off. He didn't glance towards the alligator again. It was still there though. He hadn't heard it move yet and could still sense its presence.

Without warning, the alligator charged. The trees it was in and behind, snapping, cracking into splinters, and being plowed over by the monster's sheer power and scale armored bulk.

Tristan screamed in utter terror, whirling around to face it. Leveling the three barrels of his shotgun directly at the alligator's head, he fired them all at once. The shotgun boomed like a detonating bomb. The heavy slugs slammed into the alligator right between its eyes, penetrating the armor-like scales there. The gator's blood and brain matter exploded outward as the slugs punched inward. Head rising upwards, the gator gave a screech and collapsed over onto its side. The thing's huge body lay twitching and spasming, tail swinging about wildly, smashing everything it made contact with. Tristan threw himself sideways to avoid flying splinters from a tree trunk that the dying alligator's tail struck.

The alligator's body gave a final rippling shudder and then stopped moving. Tristan stood gawking at it in disbelief. He'd actually killed the thing. His tri-barrel shotgun swung limply at his left side as his right hand came up to clasp his cheeks and rub them. Having figured he was as good as dead, this was one hell of a stunning turn of events Tristan could only credit to blind, dumb luck. It hit him that he was a hero now. He had stopped the monster killing people in the swamp and on his own too. It was too bad that Rita and Luka weren't around to see it. Like everyone else in his family, Tristan was too much of an opportunist to not be thinking already about how he could use the monster's death to his advantage. The first and most important thing was making sure that he got credit for the kill. There was no way he could get the giant gator corpse out of the swamp by himself. Hell, it would take the power of a dang truck just to move it. The gator was over twenty feet long and easily weighed close to a ton, maybe a good deal more from the heavy appearance of its armor-like scales.

A loud hissing noise drew his attention away from the gator's body.

“What in the hell?” Tristan blurted out, turning towards where the noise was coming from. As he saw its source, his eyes bugged and his mouth fell open. Not ten yards from where he stood was another gator. This one was even larger than the one he had just killed. It was sure as hell thirty feet long or more and the thing's damn shoulders and head were close to five feet above the muddy ground. He was like an infantryman in World War II standing in front of the tank that was about to take his life.

More hissing drew his attention. The giant alligator wasn't alone. There were more of the monsters, all of them massive. Tristan's mouth went dry. His shotgun was empty. There were shells in the pockets of his vest but not enough, nowhere near enough. One of the gators took a step towards him. He was surrounded. Even if he could make a run for it, gators were damn fast in short sprints. He'd never be able to get away from ones the size of these guys. Tristan closed his eyes and took a deep breath as the advancing gator lunged the rest of the way to him, closing the distance in only a few strides of its long legs. The upper part of its mouth caught the back of his skull, teeth crunching through bone and plunging into the softness of his brain, as the lower part of its mouth swung upwards. The massive gator's jaws chomped together on him severing his arms from his body and cutting his torso apart just above his sternum in an explosion of blood. What remained of his body toppled to the mud.

****

Sheriff Peterson, Cooper, and Stacia met up with several of the other search parties. Among them were a mix of deputies and state troopers. Sheriff Peterson recognized most of them: Jeffery, Henson, Zeke, Daniel, and Higgins.

Each and every one of them was armed with at least a rifle or shotgun, some with sidearms or machetes too. Their uniforms were soiled from slogging through the muddy banks and at times knee deep waters. They were all gathered on a large, clear spot of solid ground near the center of Trenton Swamp. Looking them over, Sheriff Peterson wondered how they could have missed the gator. Based on the evidence, the thing was a freaking giant. There shouldn't be any easy way for it to hide out here unless it was in the open water beyond the edge of the swamp. And out there, he had the Green Brothers crew and the Suttons both poking around. They were the best of the best. If the gator was in those waters, one of them would find it.

Most of the parties that had grouped together in the clearing were milling about smoking, guzzling water to fight the heat of the day, or gnawing on jerky. Zeke had brought a five pound bag of the stuff and was passing it out to those who wanted some.

“What are you thinking?” Stacia asked stepping up to stand next to him.

“That thing has to be out here, Stacia,” Sheriff Peterson answered. “So where the hell is it?”

“Don't worry,” she rested a hand on his shoulder, “We'll find it. Things are just taking a bit longer than we thought, that's all.”

It was at that moment, hell came calling. A series of loud crashes rang out from the side of the clearing that led deeper into the swamp. Trees were falling, pushed over and shattered by the beasts emerging from them. The alligators were all gigantic, impossibly so. The smallest was close to thirty feet in length and the largest pushing forty. Their scales were thick and armor-like, yellow eyes burning with primal rage and fury.

It was more than Jeffery and Zeke could take. The two of them ran like hell. Henson, Daniel, and Higgins led by the state trooper, Cooper, held their ground, opening fire at the approaching mutated abominations. Rifles cracked and shotguns boomed, a barrage of bullets and heavy slugs meeting the alligators head on.

"Aim for their eyes!" Sheriff Peterson yelled at the top of his lungs. From the look of the alligator, their eyes were the most vulnerable areas. With luck, a shot might go straight through them into their brains and at worst, damaging them would blind the beasts.

"Damn," he heard Stacia say. "That was some quick thinking, Sheriff, but we can't fight these things!"

Sheriff Peterson wasn't taking his own advice though. He was armed with a .50 caliber M82. The rifle was the most powerful weapon present among the searchers and he figured it could blast straight through the armor-like scales. Ignoring Stacia, he hefted the M82 to brace it against his shoulder and took aim at the head of one of the charging alligators. Sheriff Peterson's finger eased back the trigger. The M82 thundered, its recoil brutal. The alligator he was aiming at was brought to a sudden halt as the area between the eyes of the alligator disintegrated into a red mist and tiny flying fragments of shattered skull bone. Its body skidded on forward for several yards even after it dropped, carried on by its momentum.

The cacophony of gunfire continued all around Sheriff Peterson and Stacia. Bullets sparked harmlessly off thick scales. The group with them were unable to drop even a single other alligator though two of them did lose an eye. Daniel's .30-.06 reduced one to a red pulp inside its socket while Henson's 12 gauge blew a gaping hole where another gator's left eye had been. Then the tide of the battle turned on a dime as the monsters reached the group in the clearing.

An alligator snatched up Henson in its mouth, slinging him about wildly. His screams were pain filled shrieks that set Sheriff Peterson's nerves on fire. Cooper went down as one of the monsters plowed right over him, crushing him beneath its weight, a clawed foot collapsing his rib cage and sending a geyser of blood spraying out from his mouth. Daniel died as the tail of an alligator that had rushed by him caught him in the back. It struck with such force his spine broke as his body was lifted from the ground and thrown a dozen yards through the air. Higgins, wailing an insane battle cry, emptied an AK-47 into the face of an alligator that was coming directly at him like a runaway freight train. The bullets, for the most part, bounced off the scales they met there. The gator's jaws snapped at Higgins but he was able to drive sideways enough to save his life and avoid them.

"Come on!" Stacia begged. "We've got to run!"

Sheriff Peterson knew she was right. The giant gators had already taken out everyone but Higgins and themselves. Stacia launched into a full out sprint, heading back the way they had come. Sheriff Peterson hesitated only long enough to watch Higgins die as another gator came up from behind and bit him in two. Higgins' upper half vanished into its mouth leaving his lower half, spurting blood, to topple over into the mud.

A normal gator could move at around twenty miles per hour. A human can run at around twenty-eight miles per hour. They might have been able to outrun the beasts except that their increased size seemed to also have increased their speed. Sheriff Peterson knew the two of them would never escape on foot with the gators coming after them. All they could do though was try. It was either that or just give up and become gator food.

Stacia was pouring on the speed, legs pumping under her. Sheriff Peterson was straining to keep up with her. She was in a lot better shape. The only thing that saved them both were the Green Brothers crew. The trio of gator hunters were hunkered down in the trees and murk as they reached the end of the clearing. Deputy Nations was with them.

"Keep going!" Graham shouted, waving them on by, his wife and Edward with him.

Sheriff Peterson gave Graham a nod of thanks as he passed him.

Edward and Deputy Nations opened up at the approaching giant gators.

"Come and get some, you mothers!" Edward yelled, the AK-47 he was armed with blazing away on full auto. Deputy Nations' Glock cracked in rapid succession.

Looking back over his shoulder, Sheriff Peterson saw that while Deputy Nations' shots weren't doing anything to the gator, except maybe making the huge monster angrier, the rounds from Edward's AK-47 were actually doing some damage. Edward had to be using some highly illegal ammo. Scales were shot through and ripped away as bursts of bright red blood splashed outward where they struck. The gator slowed as if shocked into inaction by the wounds being inflicted on it.

Both Graham and Emily were holding their fire. Armed with shotguns, they needed to let the gators get closer before their weapons even stood a chance of hurting the gigantic monsters. That was a very bad idea. If they really made a stand, Sheriff Peterson knew the three of them were sure to die like everyone else in the search parties had.

The fastest of the charging gators came straight at the trio, closing in with impossible speed. Graham and Emily blasted it together, shotguns thundering. Emily's double barrel blast hit the gator in the side of its mouth, drawing blood and knocking loose two sword-sized teeth. Graham's hit an ineffectual angle doing little more than knocking a few scales loose from the other side of its snout.

Not even slowed, the gator rammed into Graham, its snout hitting him straight on. The impact lifted the lead hunter from the ground and flung him through the air. Landing roughly in the mud and splashing into the ankle deep, murky water of the swamp, Graham went rolling through it into the broken, protruding upward wooden stalks of small, dead bushes. They pierced his flesh, cutting into him. Graham screamed as one of them went completely through his shoulder, its red smeared end sticking out next to his face.

Deputy Nations cried out as the gator turned to him. It swiped at him with the clawed foot of its right leg. The claws as long as short swords slashed Deputy Nations opened from the bottom of his throat to his groin, leaving trails of wet redness in their wake. Deputy Nations' hands moved in an attempt to catch and hold in the coils of intestines that were pouring out from the center of his gut. As his hands filled with them, his eyes rolled up to show only whites as he passed out.

Emily turned to run and try to reach him but the enraged, giant gator jumped like a springing cat, enclosing her in its jaws, and swallowing her whole.

"You bastard!" Edward raged, whirling about as he ejected his AK-47's spent magazine and slammed a fresh one into the weapon, readying it. Edward's AK-47 roared, hosing the alligator. The ammo piercing rounds it fired tore a bloody, savaged gash along the giant gator's side. The gator bellowed in rage and pain. Its huge head swung round, burning yellow eyes locking onto Edward. He had emptied the entire new magazine into the giant gator. Edward reached to change it out but never got the chance. The gator surged forward, snapping at him. Narrowly avoiding its jaws, Edward ducked and moved under the gator in his effort to escape them. Realizing where he had disappeared to, the gator backpedaled with staggering speed. One of its huge feet came down on Edward's left leg. Bone cracked, breaking. Jagged white stabbed through skin as Edward screamed, knocked to the ground. He struggled to yank his broken leg out from under the giant gator's foot. As the foot came up, the gator moving, he succeeded.

Edward couldn't get up. His leg was too badly injured to even think about trying to stand on. He had lost his AK-47. It lay a few feet beyond his reach. Thankfully the snub nose .38 revolver he'd brought along as a back up weapon was strapped to the boot of the leg that hadn't been crushed and broken. Edward yanked the .38 free of its holster. He didn't have much hope of the revolver doing much damage against the gator's thick scales. It wasn't any more powerful than a 9mm pistol. Still, it was all that was available. Pulling back the revolver's hammer with the thumb of his right hand, Edward raised the revolver in a two handed grip. The gator had stepped away from him but it was so huge that it didn't matter. It could still get at him with its powerful jaws. Edward fired directly into the gator's open mouth. Each bullet he fired plunged into the softer tissue inside of it. Edward couldn't believe it even as it was happening but the gator recoiled from him, jaws snapping closed. His last shot hammered into and pinged away from the scales of its snout.

The .38 was now empty too and there was nothing to reload it with. Edward hurled the revolver at the gator as it surged forward again. He died instantly as the gator bit down on him, removing his head and most of his shoulders.

Graham watched helplessly, clutching the wood that was sticking out from his shoulder. With a painful heave, Graham pulled himself free of it. The action caused fresh rivers of red to run from the hole the wood left in his shoulder. His shotgun was gone, lost somewhere in the shallow water and deep mud around him. Graham still had his .44 Magnum and drew it awkwardly with his left hand. His back was covered with wounds from the mess of dead, upward pointing shafts of wood he'd landed in. None were as bad as his shoulder but they still hurt like hell.

Most of the gators were gone. They had moved on beyond where he had sat impaled, heading in the direction of the makeshift base camp. The one that had killed Edward and Emily though was very much still fixated on doing him in too. Weakly raising his .44, Graham tried to aim for the gator's right eye as it crawled towards him. His first shot went wide, not hitting the great beast at all. His second was equally ineffectual, ricocheting away from the scales of the gator's forehead. Cursing, Graham forced himself to reign in his pain and emotions in order to steady his aim for his next shot. The .44 Magnum barked again and he finally hit his target. The gator's eye blew apart in a shower of gore. Head jerking sideways in response to the pain coursing through it, the gator stopped. The giant beast shook its head for a moment and then continued forward.

Graham popped off another shot and the round actually found penetration against the scales of the gator's forehead but it was too little to stop the beast again. Graham turned to attempt to run but the gator's massive jaws closed on him. His body jerked as sword-like teeth cut into him going all the way through his body. Blood flew everywhere as the gator flung him into the air. Graham bounced along the ground as he came down. He was no longer conscious as the gator scurried up to finish him.

The sacrifice of the Green Brothers crew wasn't in vain. The distraction it caused had given Sheriff Peterson and Stacia a chance to hide from the gators and saved their lives.

Sheriff Peterson saw that Stacia was fighting

back tears as they crouched among the reeds of the swamp, waist deep in muddy water. He felt like crying himself. He had utterly failed at stopping the giant gator and gotten a hell of a lot of people killed in his attempt to boot. Neither of them spoke until the gator that ate Graham had long vanished into the distance.

"Sheriff. . ." Stacia said having composed herself.

"I know," he sighed. "I screwed up."

Stacia glared at him. "There's no way you could have known. It was hard enough to believe just one of those things existed."

"I. . .I didn't even get a count on them," Sheriff Peterson admitted.

"There were eight," Stacia commented, her voice cold.

Sheriff Peterson couldn't help but smirk. Stacia was the best damn lead deputy you could ask for, a professional to her core, who always got the job done. Knowing a compliment would only be weird, instead he grunted and just repeated the number she told him, "Eight."

"And there could be more," Stacia pointed out. "What worries mc is. . ."

"They're headed in the direction of town," Sheriff Peterson finished for her.

Stacia nodded. They both knew there wasn't anyone left to stop the monsters. Zack and the dispatchers were the only members of the department that hadn't come on the gator hunt with them.

"We've got to call in the Guard," Stacia said.

Sheriff Peterson knew she was right. He was going to have to swallow his pride and reach out to Major Jenkins. Taking out his cell, he saw that it was smashed. He must have hit it on something during all the insanity.

"Mine's dead too," Stacia held up her phone for him to see. Water was dripping out of it.

"Damn it," Sheriff Peterson scowled.

"We can use one of the car radios," Stacia suggested.

"Yeah," he agreed. "But we've got to get to them first."

"Then what are we waiting for?" Stacia challenged him and took off at a brisk but cautious jog.

Sheriff Peterson shook his head, admiring her, and then followed in her wake, once again struggling to keep up.

****

Gibson's, the small mom and pop gas station on

the northern side of Bentonville, was hopping. There were several cars at the pumps and a few other customers inside. A kid was browsing the display of retro trading cars that Jose kept near the register. His mom was in the back getting the two of them sodas. Old Frank was out on the corner, smoking a cigar like he did every day as sundown drew near. Jose couldn't help but smile. Business was good, the weather was nice, and tonight Victoria had promised to make up for their missed date night last week. Thinking about that last bit warmed his heart and his pants.

A commotion outside drew Jose out of his thoughts and caused him to turn his head towards the large windows facing the pumps. It took a moment for his brain to process exactly what his eyes were seeing because it was so unreal and messed up that it was beyond belief. That was when the screams registered in his ears.

His customers were running like panicked chickens. Three, huge, scaly things that resembled alligators were closing in on the station. One of them stepped on the hood of a parked sports car. Metal caved inward beneath its clawed foot, screeching and bending. Jose watched as old man Frank tried to make a break for it, running for his beat up, ragged pick up truck. It was a valiant effort,

Jose had to admit that. He had never seen the old man move as fast before, ever. It was a vain one too. A giant alligator slid easily into his path. Its massive mouth opened and snapped closed on the old man and just like that. . . he was dead.

The mom grabbed her son by his arm, roughly dragging him away from the display of trading cards. She started for the door that led into the parking lot. Jose saw the borderline insane terror in her eyes as she passed where he stood at the register.

"You don't wanna go out there!" Jose yelled after her but it was too late. The tiny bell above it jingled as the mother wrenched the door open and fled through it. Desperately feeling the need to do something, to save her and the kid, to protect his gas station, Jose bent over behind the counter, hands fumbling around in search of the shotgun he kept there. It was meant to deal with robbers and punks, not giant monsters.

The mother and the kid only made it a few yards before one of the alligator things intercepted them in their flight and made a meal of them. The mother was swallowed up first, the kid left clutching what was left of her arm after the rest of her vanished into the alligator's mouth. The kid was wailing like a banshee as the alligator struck again, swiping him up in its jaws.

"Holy!" Jose heard himself yelp. He had followed them outside and now skidded to a halt, facing the giant alligator that ate them. Its head was right at five feet above the ground, burning yellow eyes looking directly at him. Jose's trembling hands brought up his shotgun, leveling its barrel with the giant alligator's snout. His finger squeezed the trigger but nothing happened. Jose realized that he hadn't chambered a round.

The alligator took a step towards him. Jose was already gone though. He ran back inside his gas station's main building. The bell above the door jingling happily again as he entered. The door closed on its own behind him, swinging shut. It did nothing to stop the alligator. Its snout crashed straight through the glass of the door and the wall around it. Glass shards fell clinking like rain onto the floor as wood splintered, cracking. Hearing it all, Jose didn't even slow down his pace. He jumped, hurling himself over the counter, to crash roughly to the floor behind it.

Shelves toppled, spilling their contents, as the giant alligator dragged itself farther inside the station. Jose was grimacing and rubbing the shoulder that had taken the brunt of his weight when he landed. It hadn't broken or been dislocated but it hurt like hell. The gator's breath was nightmarish to hear as it became an angry hiss louder than the air being let out of a high pressured tire.

A puddle grew on the floor where Jose crouched, yellow, warm liquid spreading outward from between his legs. His breaths were hurried, ragged gasps, body vibrating, nerves on end. It took an almost impossible amount of effort but Jose worked the pump of his shotgun. With a cha-chunk, he chambered a slug. Knowing the register counter wasn't going to save him from the giant alligator, the thing could tear right through it effortlessly, Jose sprang up to his feet, yelling.

“Get the hell out of my store!” Jose's shotgun swung into a firing position. When he squeezed the trigger this time, the weapon boomed. Its recoil was fierce and unexpected. Jose hadn't fired the shotgun in so long that he had forgotten how fierce its kick could be. He nearly lost hold of the weapon.

The heavy slug that left the shotgun's barrel in a thunderclap of unbridled fury smashed into the alligator's snout. It tore away a few scales. The alligator rose up in response to the sudden pain. The top of its head crunched the tiles of the ceiling into tattered pieces and falling dust. Jose worked the pump of the shotgun, readying another round. The gator thudded back fully onto the floor, rushing forward. It rammed into the counter, breaking it to pieces. Jose wasn't there. He had leaped over it, making a mad dash for the exit. There was no longer a door. His feet slipped around on the glass that littered the floor. Pieces of it imbedded themselves in the soles of his shoes, some of them piercing enough to draw blood from the flesh they covered. Ignoring the pain, Jose made it by the gator, so close that his body brushed against its. He burst out in front of the station. There was no one at all left around. The other gators had wandered away too. Jose could see them in the distance. The great beasts were heading deeper into town.

Panting, covered in sweat and urine, blood inside his shoes, Jose ripped his shoes off, picking the few pieces of glass that had gone through them from the soles of his feet as best he could. A furious hiss reminded him that although the other gators might be gone the one he'd shot sure as hell wasn't. The gator partially inside the store of Jose's gas station jerked around, knocking apart a section of wall in the process.

Jose sucked in a startled breath at the sight of the giant beast coming at him again. He knew outrunning it would be impossible even if he wasn't in only blood stained socks with injured feet. The powerful shotgun in his hands was equally as useless. He'd shot the thing with it at point blank range once already and the blast barely bloodied the giant gator. Still, Jose wasn't the sort to just stand there to become gator food. Limping away from the gator as fast as he could, Jose headed directly for the pumps. The gator appeared to be in no hurry as if it saw how powerless Jose appeared to be. Each lumbering, unhurried step brought it closer.

Every instinct inside of Jose told him to run despite the pain in his feet. Jose wasn't about to do that. The huge, scaly bastard crawling towards him had wrecked his station and trashed his livelihood. He was going to make it pay. Jose worked the pump of the shotgun with a loud cha-chunk, chambering a round.

The alligator's snout was pointed directly at him. Its burning, yellow eyes were locked onto him. Jose waved for the monster to come on, ready to face it. With a furious hiss the alligator suddenly lurched forward, its massive jaws opening. Jose didn't aim his shotgun at the exposed, softer tissue within the gator's mouth though. Instead he spun his body to fire straight into the gas pump next to him. The shotgun boomed, spitting a heavy slug that ripped metal, releasing gas and gas fumes, that ignited from the sparks.

The row of pumps detonated like bombs on

synchronized timers, one blowing after the other, as everything blossomed into a growing ball of fire that spilt out into the parking lot beyond them and shot upwards into the air in something akin to the mushroom cloud made by a tactical nuke. Jose was cooked alive. Flesh boiled from his bones, sloughing away from them. His eyes popped within their sockets like bursting eggs from the intensity of the heat. The gator didn't fare any better. Its eyes were blown out from the heat too and flames washed over the front of its body, frying the huge beast where it stood.

****

The giant alligators rampaged along the streets of Bentonville, killing everyone they came across. In their wake they left crushed, overturned cars and trucks, pieces of the town's residents who had been snapped up and crunched by their massive jaws, pools of cooling blood, shattered windows and smashed walls.

Gary, Shel, and the others who had been enjoying their food, drinks, and conversation inside the diner were only just hearing the hellish chaos outside and beginning to understand that the town was no longer a safe place to be.

Shel ran to the front window, staring out of it.

"Oh God help us," she wailed.

Others were getting up from their seats to move where they could see outside as well. Gary moved with them, blinking in disbelief at what he saw. Out there, down the road, a pair of impossibly large alligators were approaching the diner. Kaiju, that was the word that popped immediately into his head. As a kid Gary watched a lot of Godzilla films. As an adult, he'd loved the Pacific Rim movies. The things outside made him think of those monsters. . . mutated, strange abominations, twisted versions of the animals they used to be. That was what the alligators outside were. Their bodies were covered in dark, armor-like scales, with occasional patches of spikes amid. Eyes burning bright like furnaces hot enough to melt steel, the giant alligators appeared to be in no hurry and utterly unconcerned about the few people still alive on the streets running and screaming, attempting to get away from them.

A pick up truck with a pair of rednecks armed with shotguns pulled directly into the alligators' path. The shotguns boomed, spitting heavy slugs that hammered into their scales. Their blasts drew blood but didn't do any real damage to the great beasts. If anything, they only served to tick them off. It was difficult to judge if the good ole boys were brave or just plain stupid.

Hissing in rage one of the alligators shot forward, ramming into the truck. Metal crunched and bent. The pick up was lifted from the road and rolled over onto its side sending the occupants of its bed flying. The driver died as a gator climbed over the truck, its weight compacting the cab, collapsing it inward. Those who had been thrown from the truck fared no better. The other giant alligator had already reached them before they could even get to their feet. It snatched the closest, flinging him up into the air before the thing's massive jaws opened again to swallow him whole. The other man was shrieking in terror, his shotgun aimed at the gator who had just chowed down on his buddy. He squeezed the weapon's trigger, firing point blank into the gator's face as it launched itself forward at him. Scales were blown from its snout and blood sprayed from the wound the heavy shell inflicted. Though the man had managed to cause the gator pain it was far from enough to save his life. The gator bit away the entire top of his body as gore was splashed all over the road.

The people inside the diner were panicking. Several of them ran for the door leading into the parking lot trying to get to their vehicles despite the dangers outside. Others raced for the rear exit, cutting through the kitchen, hoping to escape that way. Shel was jostled about by the mad rush. Gary caught her or she would have been knocked to the floor and trampled to death in the chaos. He held her tight. Shel didn't try to fight him off. Instead she pressed closer against him. He looked down into her eyes and saw the gratitude in them. She knew he had just saved her life. Then the crowd was cleared out and they were standing alone in front of the window.

Gary never went anywhere unarmed. He was wearing a concealed .45 caliber 1911 with a seven round magazine. There was no way in hell the 1911 was going to stop the monsters in the streets. The mutant alligators were enormous, their bodies well armored by thick scales like a sort of natural chain mail. Gary had brought more weapons along with him this morning but. . .they were in his car. His gut told him that trying to reach them was a very bad idea right now. He needed them though. The diner wasn't going to offer any real protection against the alligators when they were finished with the people on the streets and in the parking lot and started looking for more food.

"Thank you," Shel said as he released her.

She could tell he was focused on something from the stern expression on his face.

"You're not thinking about going out there, are you?" Shel asked, voice full of concern.

"I think I have to," Gary answered, being honest and direct, though his mind had barely processed her question.

"Why?" Shel squeaked.

"I have weapons that I think I'm gonna, we're all gonna need, in my car," Gary tapped the glass, indicting where he was parked.

"Weapons?" Shel looked confused. "Why do you have weapons in your car? Are you a hunter or something?"

Her question pulled his attention fully back to her.

"Something like that," he chuckled.

It was clear that Shel didn't know how to take his response.

"Do you really think a gun is going to do you any good against those. . .those things?" Shel challenged him.

"I don't think we're getting out of here alive without them," Gary frowned. "I've got to try."

"No," Shel tried to stop him as he started for the door, "You really don't."

She caught him by the arm. Gary shook himself loose.

"I'll be back," he promised and opened the

diner's front door. The little bell above the door jingled and then he was out in the parking lot, the door swinging closed behind him.

Without looking back at the diner and Shel, Gary ran for his car. Thankfully one of the two huge mutant gators had veered away and was chasing after a family running up the street. The other had reached the edge of the parking lot. A red headed woman who managed to get her car cranked had her foot down on the gas pedal. The vehicle roared out of its space, making a sharp turn to barrel towards the road. The problem was that she needed to pass right by the giant alligator to reach it.

The car had no chance. Despite its size the giant alligator was fast and agile enough to strike at it easily. The gator's left foot lashed out, smashing into the passenger side of the car. Metal crunched and tore, giving way to powerful muscles and claws capable of piercing it. The car was lifted from the ground and sent rolling. The car bounced, smashing into the pavement, window glass shattering and its driver screaming in terror and pain. Then she died, had to have, as the car landed fully on its roof and the top of the vehicle, no longer able to take the repeated impacts, went flat with the body below it.

Gary wasn't watching. He had reached his own car. Snatching the case he so desperately needed from it, Gary spun about. He heard the giant alligator hissing in rage and fury. He wasn't alone in the parking lot and that had saved his life. An old man stood fumbling with the keys to his truck, trying to get it unlocked. The gator went after him instead as Gary ran like hell.

Shel was waiting at the door as he made it there. She flung it open so that he could run right through into the diner. Gary turned to see the old man, or rather what was left of him. The huge monster had gobbled him up. The only signs of him were his lower legs and feet which protruded from the beast's scaly jaws.

Gary flung the case onto the closest table and opened it.

Shel gave a startled gasp at the sight of its contents. Gary hurriedly started assembling the rifle that the case held.

"What kind of gun is that?" Shel continued to gawk at the weapon and him each in turn.

"One powerful enough to make that thing out there regret coming our way," Gary promised.

"You'll never get it put together in time," Shel yelped. "That thing is. . ."

Before she could even finish her sentence the giant alligator reached the diner. Its huge snout plunged through the window sending shards of glass flying.

“Get back!” Gary yelled, diving in front of Shel to protect her as best he could. Pieces of the glass cut his skin and ripped into his back. None of them did serious damage but that didn't mean that they didn't hurt like hell. He shoved his case into her hands and then Gary whirled straight around, the rifle assembled and ready in his hands. Thundering as Gary squeezed its trigger, the rifle kicked against him. The .50 caliber round smashed point blank into the giant alligator's head. The .50 caliber round punched clean through its armor-like scales, penetrating them. It had struck deep but missed the giant beast's brain.

The giant alligator reared up its head into the ceiling of the diner. The ceiling came down in a mass of dust and debris in the section where it was struck, all around the gator's bleeding head.

Knowing he was in a fight that he couldn't win, Gary dodged the flailing gator's head as it shook about wildly from side to side. He saw Shel standing in the doorway to the kitchen, holding his case, motioning him in her direction. Gary ran towards Shel, not stopping as he reached her. Instead he shoved Shel on into the kitchen with him.

“The back door!” Gary barked.

“Over there!” Shel pointed.

"Let's go!" Gary ordered her. "That thing is going to tear straight through this place."

And based on the sounds coming closer from outside the kitchen that was exactly what the gator was doing, plunging forward like an unstoppable tank. The entire structure was becoming unstable as he and Shel made it out the back door. Behind the building, there was a jeep.

"That yours?" Gary asked, gesturing at it.

Shel shook her head. "I'm parked out front."

"It's ours now," Gary said, hopping into the driver's seat and setting to work hot wiring it.

"What are you. . .?" Shel began but then realized what was happening and shut up.

The diner shook behind them. The tip of the gator's snout rammed through its rear wall. Shel screamed. Gary hurried up.

The jeep's engine roared to life. The gator was still thrashing about inside the diner, breaking and smashing the wood of its structure. Gary didn't wait for the giant mutated thing to tear the rest of its way through. He rammed a foot down on the gas, backing the jeep out of its space and swinging it around.

"Hold on!" Gary warned Shel as the jeep thumped on the main road and he floored the accelerator.

****

Adam had been staring at the floor of the M1083. His head rose as another round of laughter chorused along the ranks of his fellow guardsmen riding in the rear with him. The five ton truck's powerful engine roared as it sped along the road into Bentonville. It was following two others exactly like it. Each carried a dozen troops and was loaded down with cargoes of heavy weapons.

"What about you, Adam?" Poe cracked. "You believe that crap they fed us?"

Adam stared at him, lost, with no idea what Poe was talking about.

"He means this freaking gator hunt," Darren chimed in. "You think it's real?"

Chad was shaking his head. "They can't really be sending us to hunt alligators. I get that this is Florida but man, come on."

"These ain't supposed to be normal gators," Poe laughed. "Weren't you guys listening? They're Godzilla babies!"

"Godzilla babies," Darren snorted. "That's awesome."

"Well, Adam?" Poe pressed him. "What's your take on it all?"

"Does it matter?" Adam shrugged. "Whatever is

in this town, if it bleeds, we'll kill it because that's our job, isn't it?"

"Man, do you always have to be so fragging dark?" Darren frowned.

The rear of the M1083 was covered so none of them saw the giant alligator which crashed through and out of the trees alongside the side of the road. The impact lifted the middle truck up and sent it rolling. Its first bounce killed most of the troops in its rear. Those in its cab died as the truck suddenly exploded, bursting into a blossoming ball of flame as the armament it was carrying detonated.

Looking back, the driver of the lead truck floored the gas and it sped on into the distance, leaving the last truck to fend for itself. Adam could hear the driver of their truck cursing and yelling as the brakes squealed. The truck nearly rolled itself but managed to come to a stop just short of where the giant alligator waited in the middle of the road. Adam and the others in the rear couldn't see it but heard the monster's vicious hissing.

"Out!" Adam shouted at the top of his lungs, springing up and running to fling himself from the rear of the M1083 truck. Adam's shoulder took the brunt of his landing on the road. Darren and Chad made it out after him but they were the only ones. The massive alligator crawled over the M1803, popping its wheels beneath its weight and fury, killing everyone else. The three of them scurried to their feet, running like hell. The giant alligator's gaze locked onto Chad. It went after him as he tried for the trees across the road from where they were.

"We gotta stop that bastard," Darren called out, slinging his M4 carbine up to brace it against his shoulder. The M4 boomed in rapid succession as he opened fire on the alligator. The bullets slammed into the scales covering the alligator's body and sparked harmlessly off, not doing more than scuffing them. They got zero penetration against the beast's natural chain mail-like armor.

The gator ignored the attack on it completely. Chad must have realized that there was no outrunning the thing on foot. He turned to make his stand, his M4 blazing. Even at point blank, straight into the gator's snout, its bullets didn't do crap. Jaws opening to snap close again with a level of speed that was almost a blur, the giant gator took Chad's arms from him. One second they were there, bracing his M4, and the next they were gone in a splash of red. Chad staggered backwards, geysers of blood spraying outward from the stumps of what remained of them. He shrieked like a dying cat in shock and pain. The gator lurched forward again, chomping on Chad again and this time pulling him up into its mouth. His severed lower legs dropped to the road as the rest of him was swallowed whole.

"Holy. . .!" Darren shouted, gawking at the gator. "It. . It just ate him!"

"Get your head out of your butt, man, or we're next!" Adam warned. They had to stop the thing but their M4s sure as hell weren't up to the task. They needed a plan.

The gator hissed, rearing up its head. Darren's M4 sprayed the underside of its throat with rounds. A few of them actually drew blood, angering the massive monster. Its head lowered, yellow eyes burning with rage locking onto Darren.

"Help!" Darren yelled, so terrified he flung his M4 aside, running for the trees at the edge of the road.

Adam took advantage of the gator's anger and fixation on Darren. Pushing his body to its limits, he poured on the speed, running up beside the gator before it could realize what he was up to. Yanking a grenade from his belt, Adam popped its pin. As he reached the gator, Adam tossed it into the thing's open mouth. The gator clamped down on it as the grenade detonated between its jaws. Wet, red clumps of tissue blew outward. Adam could see that the grenade had done more damage to the gator than just screwing up its mouth. Shrapnel from the blast must have gone up through the roof of its mouth or somehow through the back of its throat to hit its brain because the gator took only a single further step forward and then collapsed, thudding onto the road.

"Frag me! I can't believe it. You got the bastard!" Darren was literally hopping up with excitement.

"Yeah," Adam stood, trying to catch his breath, bent over with his hands on his knees.

Darren looked at the truck they had been riding in. It was utterly trashed and blood dripped from its crumpled metal wreckage. The truck that had been in the middle of the convoy continued to burn. There were no other survivors. It was just them. They both knew too that the lead truck wasn't coming back.

"What the hell do we do now?" Darren asked.

Adam knew they needed to catch up with the others. Being out here alone was just asking to be eaten and if another massive gator found them they almost certainly would be.

"We walk," Adam answered and nodded his head in the direction of the town they'd been heading towards before the convoy was attacked.

****

Shel was holding on for dear life as the jeep

swerved hard to avoid the jaws of a giant gator that had emerged from a side street to attack it. Gary managed to dodge its attack but nearly lost control of the jeep in the process. Its wheels squealing, the jeep right itself on the road.

"Shoot it!" Gary yelled at Shel.

His rifle was next to her in between them.

She snatched it up. Shel was grateful for all those times her father dragged her out hunting as a kid. The jeep streaked on down the street with the massive gator chasing after it. The gator's tail was thrashing from side to side behind it, shattering windows and caving in walls where it hit them along main street. The road wasn't great. Pot holes and other bumps jostled the jeep at random intervals. Shel raised the heavy rifle to her shoulder. It was all she could do to lift and hold it there. She dreaded the kick that was going to follow her pulling the trigger. At least aiming wasn't an issue. The gator was too freaking huge to miss and it was gaining on the jeep. Shel sucked in a breath, holding it, and did her best to get a stable aim at the monster's head.

The heavy rifle boomed. Shel yelped as its recoil was even worse than she thought it was going to be, nearly breaking the bone it was braced against. The high power bullet she fired left the rifle's barrel and hit its target. The center of the giant gator's skull collapsed inward between its eye, blood and brain matter exploding outward. The gator was stopped in its tracks by the horrid wound. Shel saw that it didn't go down though. Then she lost sight of it as Gary swung the jeep's steering wheel and the vehicle made a rough turn around a corner, heading off in a different direction.

Gary had taken a side street in the hope of dodging any other gators that might still be making their way into Bentonville. His speed was way faster than it should be on the street. The jeep's forward right tire struck a pot hole so hard that it blew.

"Frag!" Gary screamed, grappling with the steering wheel as this time there was just no hope of keeping control. The jeep veered from the road, bouncing up onto the sidewalk and was brought to a sudden stop by colliding with a streetlight, knocking it over. Thankfully it flew away from the jeep and not onto it.

Shel was slammed against the dash, ribs cracking from the impact, and then brutally flung back into her seat. The rifle she was holding went flying into the rear of the jeep.

Gary didn't fare much better. He managed to keep from breaking his nose against the steering wheel but at the price of trading it for his left arm. It took the brunt of him being hurled forward and snapped. Gary gritted his teeth at the pain coursing through him, trying to hold it together. There were none of the giant, mutant gators in sight but staying in the jeep was just asking for trouble.

Cradling his broken arm to his chest, Gary looked over at Shel. She was slumped in her seat, unconscious. Red dripped from her lips. Not good. Worse even because he was going to have to carry her. Though killing people was his line of work, Gary couldn't stomach an innocent dying, much less one that he actually liked and thought was a decent person.

Heaving himself out of the driver's seat, Gary stumbled onto the road. His first instinct was to grab his rifle from the rear of the jeep. He needed the rest of his gear too but couldn't carry it all. Gary settled for re-loading the rifle after making sure that Shel wasn't dead and was stable enough to be carried if he couldn't wake her up. Swinging the rifle over his shoulder by its strap and replacing his .45 caliber 1911 with a Desert Eagle, Gary moved around the jeep once more to make a final attempt at stirring Shel. He shouted her name, gently shook her, and finally resorted to slapping the hell out of her cheek. All that did was send blood splattering from her mouth.

"Damn it," Gary shook his head.

Reaching under Shel, he carefully pulled her from the jeep. It hurt so much with his broken arm that he nearly blacked out. Gary realized there was no way in hell he could carry her. The best he was able to manage was easing her to the road and dragging her, roughly, with great effort, away from the jeep just in case it went up. He didn't smell any gas leaking but one never knew what could happen.

Once Shel was a safe distance from the jeep, Gary stopped. He had no idea what the hell to do with her now. If he just left her and one of those monsters wandered by. . . Yet, there wasn't much else he could do. Wracking his brain for a solution, Gary looked up and down the street, spotting a van. It was sitting, parked on the edge of the street not too far away. If he could get Shel there and into it she'd be a lot better off than just lying out in the open. Accepting that there was no other choice, Gary sighed.

He bent to get a hold of Shel again but stopped. His head snapped up at the sound of an approaching siren. He could tell from the sound of it that the siren wasn't that of an ambulance or firetruck. It was a patrol car of some sort. Encountering the local authorities while carrying a rifle like the one slung on his back might create some problems Gary didn't need. Cursing his luck, he stepped out to flag the car down as it rounded a corner and came into view.

****

Sheriff Peterson and Stacia rode together in the patrol car that barreled along the road towards Bentonville, siren wailing and lights flashing. They had made contact with Sergeant Major Jenkins advising him of the situation. All the National Guard units in the area were being mobilized and on their way to the town. As soon as Bentonville came into view, it was easy to see that the giant gators had arrived ahead of them. There was chaos everywhere. Scores of cars passed them heading in the other direction, leaving town. The panicked and terrified looks on the faces of their drivers spoke volumes.

They were coming into Bentonville on a side road and entered well away from the town's main street. Stacia spotted the man first.

"Look!" She pointed at a man who appeared to be trying to move the body of a woman on the side of the road. Whether the woman was unconscious or dead, it was impossible to tell.

Sheriff Peterson's eyes bugged at the sight of the rifle the man had dangling by its strap from his back. Something about the guy wasn't right. He slammed on the brakes. The patrol car screeched to a halt in the middle of the street. It didn't matter. There was no other traffic to worry about at this point. Everyone who could had likely fled already. Leaping from the car, Stacia ran towards the man and woman.

"What happened?" Stacia asked.

"One of those giant monsters caused our jeep to wreck," the man told her.

"Just who the hell are you?" Sheriff Peterson demanded of the man as he approached him.

"You can call me Gary," the man answered.

Sheriff Peterson had been around the block enough times to know that there was no way in hell Gary was this guy's real name.

"That's quite a piece of hardware you got there," Sheriff Peterson gestured at the heavy rifle.

"Are you seriously going to ask me for a permit right now?" Gary's facial features were twisted into a furious scowl.

Ignoring the snide remark, Sheriff Peterson looked around. "I suppose the whole town is like this?"

"Yeah. Most of it I'd guess," Gary frowned. "Those things are really tearing the place apart. That begs the question, just where have you been?"

Sheriff Peterson sucked in a breath to let Gary have it but Stacia cut him off.

"We were out in the swamp trying to find and kill those things," she said. "Going in though, we had no idea that there was more than one or just how blasted tough the things are to kill. They tore apart our hunting parties like we were nothing."

"Damn," Gary shook his head.

"We've the national guard en route," Sheriff Peterson offered up, not seeing how it could hurt anything regardless of who or what this Gary guy was. "They might be here already. We were on our way to join up with them."

"How is she?" Gary asked Stacia, noticing the deputy checking Shel over again.

He had a lot of experience in the field dealing with wounds but knew that Stacia might have more actual training than he did.

"Broken ribs for sure and likely a concussion to boot," Stacia shrugged. "She needs a lot more medical help than we can give her here pronto."

"Look, Gary," Sheriff Peterson cut in, "I'm sorry about your friend there but we're going to have to leave her in your hands."

"The hell you are," Gary took a step forward.

Sheriff Peterson didn't move or even flinch.

"I'd take a moment if I was you," Sheriff

Peterson warned. "Before you do something you might just regret, son."

Gary backed down but not because he was bothered by the warning. He just didn't need the trouble and there was a hell of a lot more important stuff going on than having it out with a local sheriff he didn't even know.

"Will you two get a fragging grip!" Stacia scolded them. "This whole damn town is being eaten alive and you guys are about to start throwing punches."

"Stacia, I. . ." Sheriff Peterson stammered.

"Here's what's going to happen," she said, voice cold and firm. "You two are going to help me load Shel here into the patrol car and then I am going to get her some help. In the meantime, you can take one of the cars around here, even if you have to hot wire one, and meet up with the guard. Got it?"

"Sure," Sheriff Peterson nodded. "That's a good idea."

Gary was impressed by the attractive deputy. "Works for me."

They got Shel loaded into the car and watched Stacia turn it around, heading back out of town.

After she was gone, the two of them looked at each other.

"We should get moving," Gary said.

“Yeah,” Sheriff Peterson grunted in agreement.

Hurrying to the van he had considered loading Shel in, Gary hopped in the driver's seat.

“Hey!” Sheriff Peterson challenged him.

“Unless you know how to hot wire this thing, Sheriff, sorry, but you're riding shotgun.”

Minutes later, the van's engine roared to life.

“Where to?” Gary asked.

“Just head for the sound of screams and gunfire,” Sheriff Peterson quipped.

At first, Gary thought the sheriff was joking but then he heard them in the distance and knew he wasn't.

The van rolled out at a fast but cautious pace. Gary had learned his lesson about the giant gators coming out of nowhere.

****

Sergeant Major Jenkins found himself in command of the units trying to hold the line in Bentonville. A firing line had been hastily set up at the far end of town. He wasn't willing to risk his personnel in an attempt to save what was left of the town. His focus now was two fold: stop the blasted mutants from getting anywhere else and kill the things. He wanted them blown to pieces.

Under no delusions about the firing line of

infantrymen stopping the giant gators, even with the L.A.W.s that were deployed to several troops along it, Sergeant Major Jenkins was counting on the two tanks under his command to get the job done. They sat ahead of the firing line waiting, main guns trained towards the inner part of Bentonville. There was also air support en route but it was still nearly ten minutes out.

A giant gator rounded the corner of a distant street, glancing at the tanks. Sergeant Major Jenkins tapped his comm. and gave the order, "Light that mother up!"

He was well aware that it was a risk to open fire on just one of the things. If they succeeded in taking it down, doing so might scare off the others. It was a risk he was willing to take, though.

The .50 caliber commander's guns of the two Abrams let loose at the giant gator. The heavy rounds punched straight through the thick armor of its scales. The gator whined in pain and tried to turn around but doing so only exposed more of its body. Bullets slashed a train of red gore all the way from its head to the start of its tail. With a final shriek, the giant gator collapsed.

A chorus of cheers arose from the ranks of infantrymen in the firing line. Sergeant Major Jenkins allowed himself a smile. Maybe this wasn't going to be so difficult after all.

The moment of victory was brief. Without warning, a pack of other gators came spilling from the town towards the tanks and the firing line. The tanks' .50 calibers sprang back into action. They managed to drop two more of the monsters but the gators reached them and things, hardcore, went to crap. A gator locked its jaws on the barrel of the right Abram's main gun. Metal squealed as the gator wrenched the barrel, bending it sideways. The gator released the barrel, damage done, and went after the treads of the tank next as if the thing somehow knew what they were and how they functioned. It didn't. It was merely an easy place to bite from the position it was in and bad luck for the tank's crew.

A pair of other gators hit the second Abrams like a tidal wave of savage force, upending it with their snouts. The tank went up and over, slamming down onto its top. The gunner at its .50 was killed instantly, reduced to little more than a red smear. The two gators instantly tore into the overturned tank, biting and clawing at its armor. Sparks flew from their vicious attack and one managed to rip the right side treads free.

To their credit, most of the guardsmen on the firing line didn't run. They held their positions, a cacophony of automatic gunfire erupted. Aside from the occasional lucky shot that stung the gators, the barrage didn't do anything to stop the monsters.

The L.A.W.s and RPGS among the ranks of the men fighting for their lives did do some damage. A gator died as a missile streaked into its open maw. Its head blew apart in a shower of gore. Another took a hit that sent it staggering, a huge bloody hole gouged in one of its shoulders. A gator got hit twice, losing its left leg and then getting a gaping hole blasted in its upper back. That was the extent of fighting back the national guardsmen were able to do before the battle became a mixture of a massacre and a rout. The troops on the firing line broke and ran.

Giant gators moved among the soldiers, snapping them up, trampling them beneath clawed feet, and cutting them down like wheat slashed by scythes with their thrashing tails. Men and women died screaming by the dozens.

Sergeant Major Jenkins was forced to retreat as well. He dropped into the passenger seat of the jeep he'd been watching the battle from, thumping the dashboard in a gesture to tell his driver to get them the hell away from the giant gators. His only hope now was the inbound air strike would succeed where his troops on the ground had failed.

The jeep shot backwards as the driver floored the gas. It wasn't fast enough though. A giant alligator came crawling at a dead out sprint towards the vehicle snaring its front with powerful jaws. The hood caved in, teeth pierced metal, and the jeep was lifted partly from the roadway, only its rear wheels still making contact. Sergeant Major Jenkins flung himself out, hitting the asphalt with a loud thud. The move might have saved him but the jeep blew, the explosion engulfing him, the driver, the jeep, and the giant alligator's head.

Sheriff Peterson and Gary arrived at the edge of town just in time to see it happen.

****

"Holy hell!" Sheriff Peterson bellowed as he slammed on the van's brakes. It skidded roughly to a halt nearly overturning into a roll. Gary caught himself to avoid being flung into the dashboard.

The scene ahead of them was like something from a nightmare. It looked as if all of the giant gators had gathered into a single pack. They were rampaging through a unit of national guardsmen who were dying in droves to the beasts. Bodies of the dead were strewn about everywhere. Some were bitten in half, others missing limbs, and several crushed to red stains on the asphalt.

There were two tanks. Both of them were disabled and no longer in the fight. The gators hadn't escaped taking some losses too. Several giant corpses lay amid the chaos. A burning jeep with a dead gator pretty much on top of it sat at the far rear of where everything was going down.

The number of the giant gators were more than Sheriff Peterson could believe. He'd thought at most there were only eight. Before his eyes though, not even counting the dead ones, were over a dozen of the monsters.

"We are so screwed," Sheriff Peterson muttered.

"Wait!" Gary yelled, pointing at something in the sky.

Sheriff Peterson saw them, five attack helicopters closing fast.

"Those are Apache AH-64E Guardians," Gary said. "They'll tear those bastard things apart!"

Sheriff Peterson sure as hell hoped so.

"Those copters have 30mm chain guns designed to be used against armor and fortified bunkers. They look to be rigged out with Hellfire missiles too," Gary explained excitedly.

The copters came in hot on a strafing run, their chain guns blazing. The giant, mutant gators reeled as a rain of armor piercing rounds fell upon them. Bright red blood splattered all over the place. The gators hissed and chirped in distress and terror. An attack from above was something that took the great beasts completely off-guard.

A gator reared up as a hail of bullets from an Apache dug a deep trail over its back from its tail to its head before flopping to the ground dead. Another had its head pulped by bursts of concentrated fire. By the time the Apache's run was over and the copters were pulling up and preparing to swing around again, six of the giant gators were no more.

Hissing in rage, a giant gator jumped into the air at one of the lower flying Apaches. Its body straightened out, powerful legs thrusting the giant gator upwards. The gator caught the Apache in its wide jaws. They snapped shut, detonating several of the missiles the copter was armed with. The copter became a blossoming ball of flame. The giant gator's head disintegrated. Bloody fragments of meat and bone span away from the blast along with the metal bits of the copter itself. Its headless body fell back to the road, cracking the asphalt from the force of its impact.

The other copters quickly pulled up putting more distance between themselves and the ground. Sheriff Peterson wagered none of their pilots would make the mistake of coming in too close again.

Pouring on speed, the Apaches continued on

before swooping around to turn towards the gators and let loose a fresh hell upon them - Hellfire missiles. The missiles streaked from the copters into the monsters. A gator took one in the center of its body. The gator burst like an over ripe melon, intestines exploding out in every direction as it quite literally blew apart. Another gator was slain as a missile struck the asphalt and chunks of it were flung up like huge bullets that ripped and tore through the armor of its scales.

In a matter of seconds it was all over. The giant gators were all dead or lying mortally wounded, bleeding out. Their job finished, the Apaches rose higher in the sky flying away in the direction they had originally appeared from.

Sheriff Peterson and Gary watched them go from where they stood in front of the van they had arrived in.

"Wow," Gary muttered. "They really wrecked those bastards."

Elbowing Gary in the ribs to shut him up, Sheriff Peterson whispered, "Not all of them. Look over there!"

Gary sucked in a startled breath as he saw the gator. It was smaller than the others but the monster was still easily over twenty feet from head to tail. The spiked gator was crawling out of the smashed large, forward facing windows of a grocery store. The thing had taken cover within it as the Apaches attacked. Its body was far more heavily covered in the weird spikes that spotted the scales of its brothers and sisters. Its eyes burned a hot yellow full of primal rage.

"We've got to kill that thing," Sheriff Peterson said rushing back to snatch a pump action shotgun he had brought along from the van. "We can't let it get away."

"Not my problem," Gary shrugged. "I'll be seeing you around, Sheriff."

"Oh it's your problem alright, *Gary*," Sheriff Peterson emphasized his name. "If you don't help me stop that thing I can promise that whoever or whatever you really are won't be staying a secret."

Gary froze. He looked at the sheriff. It was clear Peterson meant what he said.

"I could just kill you," Gary smirked. "In all this mess, it wouldn't be hard at all to make sure no one ever knew that I'd done it."

"You could try," Sheriff Peterson stared him down.

Shaking his head, Gary laughed.

"What?" Sheriff Peterson asked, confused.

"I must be getting soft, Sheriff," Gary sighed. "Come on. Let's go end that thing."

****

Like Old West gunfighters, Gary and Sheriff Peterson walked along the street towards the spike-covered alligator. The thing was busy tearing at the corpse of a larger alligator in savage hunger and didn't see them.

"I'll get that thing's attention and you send it to hell with that rifle of yours, got it?" Sheriff Peterson asked. "We're only likely to get a single shot at this."

"Don't worry," Gary grinned, "I got it."

Together they kept walking until they were only yards away from the alligator.

"Hey, you bastard!" Sheriff Peterson shouted. "Suck on this!"

His shotgun came up thundering. The slug it fired struck the spiked alligator just above its tail. The shot didn't do any real damage to the beast. It certainly got its attention though. Hurling itself around with near impossible speed, the spiked alligator charged them. Gary was ready for it though. His finger squeezed the trigger of his rifle as he aimed for where he hoped the gator's brain was.

The high powered round found its target. Bone shattered and gave way as the bullet entered the gator's skull and then burst outward at an upwards angle in a spray of gore and bone fragments. The burning yellow in the spiked gator's eyes dimmed and went out. Its legs went limp and the gator dropped where it stood.

Sheriff Peterson and Gary watched the thing twitching in its death throes. Gary shot it again, once more aiming for its head. The second shot did more cosmetic damage to the gator's head than the first, caving its already compromised skull. Then finally, the entire street was quiet and still. There were only the two of them and the dead gator.

****

A week later, Gary sat on his front porch watching the sunset. Everything that happened in the town of Bentonville and its surrounding swamps had been quite eloquently covered by the powers that be. All the deaths were blamed on a terrible chemical spill. Neither he nor the sheriff was happy with that but they both understood there was nothing that could really be done about it. If they came forward with the truth, they would be discredited and hushed up, one way or another. Gary had done some hushing of that sort in his prior career.

On the upside, there were no signs at all that any

of the mutant gators were still around. It seemed all of the things had been successfully wiped out. Gary briefly considered packing up and moving somewhere far away to start over again but couldn't bring himself to do it. He had a reason to stay in Bentonville now and her name was Shel. The two of them had really hit it off.

Glancing at his watch, Gary saw that she should be arriving any minute. He had dinner ready and waiting inside. Getting up from his rocking chair, Gary moved to stand at the edge of the porch. The sky was a beautiful shade of purple.

He was smiling like an idiot when the boards of the porch next to where he stood were shattered as something white covered in scales with gleaming teeth punched through them. A quick bite severed his left leg at the knee. Gary howled in pain, dropping to find himself face to snout with a man-sized, albino alligator. Its eyes were full of rage as the gator surged forward to tear out his throat in an explosion of blood. Gary's mind barely had time to process what it was that killed him before his life was over and he became the white alligator's early evening snack.

The End

Eric S Brown is the author of numerous book series including the Bigfoot War series, the Psi-Mechs Inc. series, the Kaiju Apocalypse series (with Jason Cordova), the Crypto-Squad series (with Jason Brannon), the Jack Bunny Bam series, and the A Pack of Wolves series. Some of his stand alone books include Snarl, Sasquatch Nightmare, Manhunt, Cryptid Park, War of the Worlds plus Blood Guts and Zombies, Casper Alamo (with Jason Brannon), Sasquatch Island, Day of the Sasquatch, Bigfoot, Crashed, World War of the Dead, Last Stand in a Dead Land, Sasquatch Lake, Kaiju Armageddon, Megalodon, Megalodon Apocalypse, Kraken, Alien Battalion, The Last Fleet, and From the Snow They Came to name only a few. His short fiction has been published hundreds of times in the small press in beyond including markets like the Onward Drake and Black Tide Rising anthologies from Baen Books, the Grantville Gazette, the SNAFU Military horror anthology series, and Walmart World magazine. He has done the novelizations for such films as Boggy Creek: The Legend is True (Studio 3 Entertainment) and The Bloody Rage of Bigfoot (Great Lake films). The first book of his Bigfoot War series was adapted into a feature film by Origin Releasing in 2014. Werewolf Massacre at Hell's Gate was the second of his books to be adapted into film in 2015. Major Japanese publisher, Takeshobo, bought the reprint rights to his Kaiju Apocalypse series (with Jason Cordova) and the mass market, Japanese language version was released in late 2017. Ring of Fire Press has released a collected edition of his Monster Society stories (set in the New York Times Best-selling world of Eric Flint's 1632). In addition to his fiction, Eric also wrote a pop culture column featured in Altered Reality Magazine for many years. Eric lives in North Carolina with his wife and two children where he continues to write tales of the hungry dead, blazing guns, and the things that lurk in the woods.

SEVERED**PRESS**

@severedpress
/severedpress

Check out other great

Cryptid Novels!

J.H. Moncrieff

RETURN TO DYATLOV PASS

In 1959, nine Russian students set off on a skiing expedition in the Ural Mountains. Their mutilated bodies were discovered weeks later. Their bizarre and unexplained deaths are one of the most enduring true mysteries of our time. Nearly sixty years later, podcast host Nat McPherson ventures into the same mountains with her team, determined to finally solve the mystery of the Dyatlov Pass incident. Her plans are thwarted on the first night, when two trackers from her group are brutally slaughtered. The team's guide, a superstitious man from a neighboring village, blames the killings on yetis, but no one believes him. As members of Nat's team die one by one, she must figure out if there's a murderer in their midst—or something even worse—before history repeats itself and her group becomes another casualty of the infamous Dead Mountain.

Gerry Griffiths

CRYPTID ZOO

As a child, rare and unusual animals, especially cryptid creatures, always fascinated Carter Wilde. Now that he's an eccentric billionaire and runs the largest conglomerate of high-tech companies all over the world, he can finally achieve his wildest dream of building the most incredible theme park ever conceived on the planet... CRYPTID ZOO. Even though there have been apparent problems with the project, Wilde still decides to send some of his marketing employees and their families on a forced vacation to assess the theme park in preparation for Opening Day. Nick Wells and his family are some of those chosen and are about to embark on what will become the most terror-filled weekend of their lives—praying they survive. STEP RIGHT UP AND GET YOUR FREE PASS... TO CRYPTID ZOO

Check out other great

Cryptid Novels!

P.K. Hawkins

THE CRYPTID FILES

Fresh out of the academy with top marks, Agent Bradley Tennyson is expecting to have the pick of cases and investigations throughout the country. So he's shocked when instead he is assigned as the new partner to "The Crag," an agent well past his prime. He thinks the assignment is a punishment. It's anything but.Agent George Crag has been doing this job for far longer than most, and he knows what skeletons his bosses have in the closet and where the bodies are buried. He has pretty much free reign to pick his cases, and he knows exactly which one he wants to use to break in his new young partner: the disappearance and murder of a couple of college kids in a remote mountain town.Tennyson doesn't realize it, but Crag is about to introduce him to a world he never believed existed: The Cryptid Files, a world of strange monsters roaming in the night. Because these murders have been going on for a long time, and evidence is mounting that the murderer may just in fact be the legendary Bigfoot.

Gerry Griffiths

DOWN FROM BEAST MOUNTAIN

A beast with a grudge has come down from the mountain to terrorize the townsfolk of Porterville. The once sleepy town is suddenly wide awake. Sheriff Abel McGuire and game warden Grant Tanner frantically investigate one brutal slaying after another as they follow the blood trail they hope will eventually lead to the monstrous killer. But they better hurry and stop the carnage before the census taker has to come out and change the population sign on the edge of town to ZERO.

SEVEREDPRESS

@severedpress
/severedpress

Check out other great

Cryptid Novels!

Hunter Shea

LOCH NESS REVENGE

Deep in the murky waters of Loch Ness, the creature known as Nessie has returned. Twins Natalie and Austin McQueen watched in horror as their parents were devoured by the world's most infamous lake monster. Two decades later, it's their turn to hunt the legend. But what lurks in the Loch is not what they expected. Nessie is devouring everything in and around the Loch, and it's not alone. Hell has come to the Scottish Highlands. In a fierce battle between man and monster, the world may never be the same. Praise for THEY RISE : "Outrageous, balls to the wall...made me yearn for 3D glasses and a tub of popcorn, extra butter!" – The Eyes of Madness "A fast-paced, gore-heavy splatter fest of sharksploitation." The Werd "A rocket paced horror story. I enjoyed the hell out of this book." Shotgun Logic Reviews

C.G. Mosley

BAKER COUNTY BIGFOOT CHRONICLE

Marie Bledsoe only wants her missing brother Kurt back. She'll stop at nothing to make it happen and, with the help of Kurt's friend Tony, along with Sheriff Ray Cochran, Marie embarks on a terrifying journey deep into the belly of the mysterious Walker Laboratory to find him. However, what she and her companions find lurking in the laboratory basement is beyond comprehension. There are cryptids from the forest being held captive there and something...else. Enjoy this suspenseful tale from the mind of C.G. Mosley, author of Wood Ape. Welcome back to Baker County, a place where monsters do lurk in the night!

Printed in Dunstable, United Kingdom

64907521R00080